Published by Ad Hoc Fiction.
www.AdHocFiction.com

Purchasing Information:
Paperback available from www.AdHocFiction.com
E-book available from all usual outlets.

Printed Worldwide.
First Printing 2020.

ISBN paperback 978-1-912095-10-0
ISBN e-Book 978-1-912095-09-4

RESTORE TO FACTORY SETTINGS

Bath Flash Fiction Volume Five

Forward

We're excited to introduce *Restore to Factory Settings*, the fifth anthology from the Bath Flash Fiction Award – 136 flash fictions of 300 words and under by authors from the three Awards in 2020. This year we received, in total, 4235 entries from 49 different countries around the world:

Australia; Austria; Bangladesh; Belgium; Brazil; Cameroon; Canada; China; Cyprus; Czech Republic; Croatia; Denmark; France; Germany; Greece; Hong Kong; Hungary; India; Indonesia; Ireland; Israel; Italy; Japan; Kazakhstan; Kuwait; Lesotho; Luxembourg; Malaysia; Mexico; Mozambique; Netherlands; New Zealand; Nigeria; Norway; Philippines; Portugal; Qatar; Romania; Senegal; Singapore; South Africa; Spain; Sri Lanka; Sweden; Switzerland; Taiwan; United Arab Emirates; United Kingdom; United States.

Thank you very much to everyone who entered. 2020 has been such a challenging year, but this has not deterred writers from producing stories that astonished our reading team with their creativity and inventiveness. There were many close calls for the long lists of fifty in each round of the Award.

This year, the three judges for the Awards were, writer, editor, teacher and National Flash Fiction Day, UK Director, Santino Prinzi from the UK; poet, prose writer, editor and teacher, Mary Jane Holmes who divides her time between the UK and the US and Nod Ghosh, a writer, artist, teacher and editor from New Zealand. They all agreed the stories they read were of a very high standard and covered many different subjects and themes in interesting and challenging ways:

Santino Prinzi wrote:
"Reading the fifty long listed flashes I received, I knew these stories were – are – loved by their authors. But they were also so much more than that. Each story had its own distinct quality, its own voice, its own style and structure. Each had sentences I underlined and words I circled. Not knowing what I was looking for, I found everything."

Mary Jane Holmes wrote:
"... I read a lot of flash and when I read the BFFA long list I thought there had to be some mistake, I must be reading the shortlist instead of the long list, so high was the quality of the work I was looking at. This made the judging process incredibly enjoyable on the one hand – to see so much variety, so much stimulating and original work, a wonderful willingness to experiment, and on the other hand, so difficult to choose."

Nod Ghosh wrote:
"It's been a pleasure reading these pieces, the quality indicates how well contributors craft their stories, producing shining gems of literature that show this genre is not alone alive and well, but is thriving. The range of topics and styles on offer show practitioners of this form can still find something fresh or interpret ideas in a novel way."

We greatly appreciate all three judges for their work in reading the stories, making their selections, writing interesting and constructive comments on the winners and for working to our tight schedule. You can read their full reports on our website, bathflashfictionaward.com. The fifteen placed stories from the three Awards are at the beginning of the book, followed by the remainder of the short list (judge's selection) and then the rest of the long listed stories (editor's choice). So many brilliant and varied stories to read.

A further thanks to the BFFA team who love the flash fiction form and are happy to read stories throughout the submission period and very intensively during the last busy weeks.

This year, the title, *Restore to Factory Settings,* is from one of two excellent stories in the anthology by UK writer, J A Keogh and it ends this collection. We think it's a fitting title for these times. Nothing stays the same, either in the world, or in fiction. We can always begin things again, hopefully.

We look forward to reading more wonderful flash fictions on all subjects in the 2021 entries.

Jude Higgins
BFFA founder
November 2020.

Contents

Sharon Telfer

Eight Spare Bullets

1

The front windows refuse to shut. The house droops, as after a stroke.

They drink in the kitchen. Under the slanting floor, they catch the trickle of thaw.

2

Everything here is the northernmost. Town, church, store, pub. The last.

She replays her field recording, bowhead whales, all booming fuzz and feedback.

"Harmonics!" Erik applauds. "That's freeform jazz."

The last blues festival.

3

He softens in her mouth. *It's okay*, she whispers, though it's not. She'll be gone six weeks.

From the boat, she had watched an iceberg tumble, head over heels, like a clumsy toddler. Not playing, but dying.

Erik kisses her, has to go. Husky safari, tomorrow's fresh batch of tourists.

He kisses his dogs too. Erik loves his dogs.

4

Everything slides. The wooden stilts sink beneath the houses. A landslip buries the play park. The ground heaves the dead from their graves, sends coffins tobogganing down the road.

She wakes. Remembers. Not a dream. Last summer.

5

Her breath freezes in her nostrils.

Reindeer antlers heap by the roadside. They gleam in her torchlight, like bleached coral.

6

Time loses its way in the permanent dark. The once-white mountain looms black. Deep below, one million seeds – a world's worth – lie buried. They called it the doomsday vault, fast as a dragon's hoard. Nine years after opening, meltwater has already flooded in.

7

Beware of polar bears.

A mother and cubs wandered down this street, past the last post office, the last chocolaterie.

If you leave town, you must take a gun and eight spare bullets.

8

The plane spins her back into sunrise.

She thumbs up a clip. Erik dancing with his dogs, a circling, shuffling waltz.

At the northernmost, there more polar bears than people. If you meet a bear, pull back quietly.

Fiona Perry

Sea Change

He arrives breathless with excitement, clutching a thick plastic bag bulging with shells. At the kitchen table, he points to the bag and tells me they fattened up over winter. At first, they settled as larvae on ropes, before growing to half the length of a thumb, ready to be stuffed like sausage meat into casings known as *socks*. The runt grouped with the runt, the alpha with the alpha to prevent unfair competition. I imagine it – the swaying of the long mesh tubes – the seething growth of it. I tell him all of this is wonderful, resisting the urge to remind him he is in fact dead. He smiles and asks me to pour vodka for us into his old reko tumblers which have appeared on my countertop. He says that once the molluscs reach full maturation, they are able to travel outside of the sock – by attaching a byssal thread from their beard to an anchor and then shortening it to move. He finds this both funny and moving. Soon afterwards, he says, the sock collapses into the centre of the column. *Collapses into the centre of the column,* he repeats. He wipes his mouth with his hand. I am standing beside the stove now, frying diced onion and garlic in the big pasta pot I misplaced years ago, into which I squirt tomato paste, let it sizzle, splash in vodka, warm water and cream. He tips the mussels from the bag into the pot, I sprinkle in sea salt and clamp on the lid. He explains that this is where he has been all along, looking after these creatures. His face soft like a monk's, he announces he must leave after dinner because new larvae always require his attention out in the ocean.

Johanna Robinson

Blessings, 1849

You remember how you counted your steps as you planted: one step, one potato. The years God gave you babies, the steps were smaller with the weight in your belly, on your back. The years He took them away before you could count a single breath, the steps were smaller still, the potatoes fighting for space and soil. Those years, you ate such small potatoes.

In the barn, in the dark, you'd count the rungs, so you knew how far up you were, how far down. Sometimes you felt you could climb forever, out through the roof-hatch, inching up the sky until your hands brushed theirs, tiny, grasping.

You'd count stitches and rows: hats, jackets, bootees. Seed stitches, garter stitches, cable, plaited, travelling vine. Casting on, and on, and on.

You'd count the steps around the kitchen table, through colic, through cries, until the minutes unravelled, flat like ribbons, and your heels blistered.

Every morning you'd count:
> the eggs and then the chickens, and
>> in the evening, brushstrokes, dividing your hair, weaving it into one heavy rope, and
>>> at night, stretchmarks like rungs across your belly.

And now there are no potatoes for anyone, you take uncertain steps, quay to jetty. You walk gently, the baby's head on your shoulder. You walk steady, like you used to carry eggs.

You lean on the ship's rail, wet with spray, your faces already salty. On the quay, people wave, and you wave back as though you know them. The children count down and other passengers join in. The rope sags, like a stitch dropped. You clap, clasp hands, cast off. You leave behind bone, blood and eggshell, but your history is more than that; it is ploughed through you all. You count the days, knots, miles until land. You will reap again.

Simon Cowdroy

The Dissolution of Peter McCaffrey

Heat-ravaged rivets explode off the corrugated iron roof of our milking shed like corks from shaken champagne bottles.

A long drought wind scalds in from the north and the thermometer leaves 50 behind as pitiless gusts scour every nook of the farm. No easy pickings to be found; all that could be taken is long gone.

Dad wasn't a man you made a promise to lightly, his plea for me to stay burdened with the heft of eight generations. I crane my neck, spot his cross, remember the soil being so unyielding we used up all our dynamite. Not enough time or faith left over for funerals, so his pension cheque still ghosts in.

I lost Annie to the highway a week back. No goodbyes, only the midnight creak of our front door, the bloom of liberated fuel as her car engine fired.

Well rid of her two-faced grace, the lies that fell from those blue eyes as acid rain, but I can't seem to shake that afternoon before she left. The brutal whisper of, "Pete, we're in this together," as my tired, fractured head folded into her shoulder.

Joe at the Co-Op rings. The water tankers aren't coming. He chews my ear about it being the start of Australia's climate change but sure feels to me like we're already at the end of everything.

Three hundred cattle are all that remain and I've enough feed to get half through next week. The cull is almost a familiar dance now. I never remember grabbing my gun; never forget to keep a bullet in the chamber after it's done.

I'm not a brave man, and if soft bovine eyes ever boiled over in accusation it would unbind me. Turns out, their gratitude is what keeps me awake.

Hannah Storm

The species of pangolin compromise their own order: Pholidota

Pholi – A folly is something stupid.
Dota – She's learning phonics at school. This is how she would spell *daughter*.

He said I was *fucking stupid*. Ordered me to get rid of it. I cradled my belly's soft shell as it grew.

'Pangolin' comes from the Malay 'pengguling', loosely meaning something that rolls up.

Later I stuffed into a rucksack all we needed to survive, hiding our future beneath my bed. I curled up by her cot.

Special glands near the pangolin's anus secrete a pungent fluid as a defence mechanism.

Now the court toilet smells of the fear of losing my child.

That last night, he came home drunk. I'd not showered for two days between the feeding, burping, changing, rocking, cooking. He hissed at me when I begged him to be quiet.

You smell ripe. He tore at my clothes. *Why can't you make a fucking effort?* Pinned me to the bed. Cried when he came. Then she cried too. By the time I had settled her, he was snoring. The room reeked of shame.

Pangolins are nocturnal animals. Their shells made of keratin the same substance as human hair and nails.

In the show I scrubbed myself raw, let the water sear my scalp. Impossible to feel clean.

The mother curls up around the baby pangolin if she senses danger.

He left for work. Then we left. I clasped her to me, promising he would not hurt us again.

Now I hear my name, calling me to Court.

The endangered pangolin is the world's most trafficked animal; its body parts are sold as a delicacy or used for their mythical healing properties.

When my daughter is older, I will teach her how to protect herself. One day I will explain what being endangered really means.

Tara Isabel Zambrano

Mother, Before

Before, my mother settled my twin sister and me every morning in a neighbor's front yard and boarded a bus to a local bottling plant, in her powder blue uniform, her hair pulled back so hard her veins showed. We read comics with missing pages, stripped our dolls to the sun.

At the filling station, my mother watched the slosh of juices into empty bottles, her nails rubbed raw working labels, the glue peeling the skin of her finger pads. No windows, stark lights. Sealed cans holding the fruit piss. Before my mother understood the difference between acids, caustics, living and suffering, she was moved to the water treatment center where she cleaned the vents, scrubbed the floors, the chlorine, settled on her skin, in her eyes, and in her hair, made her sterile. Before the factory swallowed her each day and spit out at night, a dry seed, my mother was glass, my mother was an orange wreathed in luscious peels, my mother was sun's magma. Before, my mother's name was Anna, and the payment slips called her Lee, the last name of my father who fled to Florida with his girlfriend, his memory a blooming wound at the back of her throat. She pushed her fingers inside to pluck it, puked blood.

Before, my mother untangled the kinks in our bone black hair, kept locks of it in her purse. Before, she smelled us and scrutinized our faces, knowing how each of us looked from the day of our birth, rooted to her dowager womb by our breath placenta. Before she hibernated, before she milked tears that couldn't fix her chlorinated lungs. Before she became our child, her lips pressed against the wall, her mouth plastered. Before she crumbled into ash without a trail of soot.

Christina Dalcher

Dressage

And she rides.

She prances the beast sideways, backwards, up, down, feet in the air, falling, balancing, tumbling, perfect circles carved on the red dirt of Spain. Ten years, twelve years, fourteen. Fly a thousand miles from home. Fly south, jump left, skip right. One, two, three. Uno, dos, tres. Één, twee, drie.

And they watch.

Pay your thirty euros; see the Andalusian horses dance. Piaffe, pirouette, travers. Impossible, unnatural gymnastics. Watch the braids in their manes and the flowers in their tails. Watch the girl, ten years, twelve years, fourteen. Watch her fly one last time.

And he bucks.

You can lead a horse to water, but you can't make him dance. Because a beast is a beast, mare or stallion, Arabian or Andalusian. To its ears, Ravel and Offenbach and Sousa make noise, not music. Once a day, twice on Thursday, thunderclap roars of *olé-bravo-jolly good show*. So tired. Weary of spurs and bits and reins and weight.

And she breaks.

She breaks in the middle and at the ends, bones flattening, nerves singing. She breaks sideways and backwards, young flesh sinking into old earth. She dreams a dream of gold, silver, bronze. She wakes.

And they gasp.

Pobrecita-poor dear-die arme-shame-tragedia-so young. Dangerous beast-willful-cattivo-too green. Mobiles ping as news travels. This is Thursday. Next show at three o'clock.

And she mends.

At the sea, she sits, legs bound in plaster, braids in her hair. She sees the wild ponies lope and trot and gallop. Sees their manes free of flowers, sees their legs naked of wraps. Riderless, they fly to the rhythm of wind and waves. When they come to nuzzle her wounds, she wonders, Who is the trainer, and who is the trainee?

Sam Payne

The Man You Didn't Marry

The police meet you after your night shift at Sunshine Care to tell you they're concerned for your safety. They found the man you didn't marry outside your house at four am. In his car, black bags, rope and a crowbar. They tell you they're sorry, but they can't hold him.

The locksmith talks about Brexit as he rips out the deadbolt and replaces it with a shiny new one. When he leaves, you barge your shoulder into the door just to make sure it doesn't give. But in the night you wake to the smell of Joop and the man you didn't marry is pushing his knuckles into your clavicle and telling you he loves you. His saliva gathers in the corners of his mouth and the white froth reminds you of tide bubbles and you focus on this as he throttles you. You lose consciousness and your body becomes a stingray slipping into saltwater.

You survive because you're lucky or at least that's what people say. You move cities, rent a different house every six months and clean everything continuously. You're happy that you have things in order. Until the therapist tells you perfectionism is a sign of unhealed trauma. When you get home, you throw Bolognese sauce at the walls, empty the cutlery drawer onto the lino and chuck your clothes out of the window until you're satisfied this chaos is proof that you're fine. But every time you sleep you're sinking into a cold, dark ocean. Submerging deeper and deeper, the saltwater strips your flesh until there's nothing left and when your skeleton rests on rippled sand, the man you didn't marry scoops you up. He polishes your bones until you shine like teeth and he keeps telling you he'll never ever let you go.

Jan Kaneen

The White Dwarf

It's months into lockdown, and Clayton's showing Thelma how to train their new state-of-the-art telescope onto the crow-black Tennessee sky. He twists the eyepiece to trap the distant white glow from a small dying star, but it's tricky capturing the faint luminosity emitted by degenerate-electron matter, and he doesn't want to seem unfocussed in front of his wife, so he bends to the lens and tries real hard to sharpen the image – sees the old wooden swing on his granddaddy's porch, a curl of Thelma's once corn-coloured hair, remnants of his long-passed mamma's last apple pie, a Thanksgiving turkey, Uncle Sam's stern white face, flickering footage of Neil Armstrong taking one giant leap, a bucket of hot chicken, Johnny Cash singing *Ring of Fire*, a bottle of Jack, his old CB radio, the penultimate episode of Dukes of Hazzard, *Resisting Arrest* as a black-and-white headline, a nest of wasps, the Twin Towers tumbling, his Smith and Wesson, that Ku Klux Klan robe and hood he saw years ago in Uncle Frank's drycleaners hanging up under a see-through plastic covering, the faces of three little kids in an SUV watching their daddy get shot six times in the back, a manacled captive under an officer's knee pleading for his mamma and his life gasping I can't breathe, I can't breathe, I can't breathe, I can't breathe.

Clayton looks away, straightens himself up, stares out into the unfathomable sheet of night-time sky – the vast blackness of it – then asks Thelma if she'd care to take her turn.

"You okay, Honey?" she says, taking in his blanched white cheeks and tight, thin lips.

"I'm fine," he drawls, "Ain't nothing." Then he gazes into her blue-sky eyes and creases his face into half a smile. "Leastwise, nothing for us to worry about."

Claire Powell

Valentine

The man steps out of his car.

Tomasz remains where he is, both hands on the wheel, as though still moving.

It's black outside, but they've stopped on the high street, beneath a yellow lamp. There's a McDonald's on the corner, brightly lit, open.

Moments earlier, while pulling out, something had caught Tomasz's eye: a gift shop filled with teddy bears and glossy heart-shaped balloons. It seemed surreal at first, but now he realises, of course: Valentine's Day.

The man bends down, picks up his wing mirror.

Tomasz remembers the card Lena once made him. A photo of them in bed, their faces close, pretending to sleep. Stupid really – he'd taken it himself. Had held his arm up high, touched his thumb to the button, closed his eyes before it flashed. *To the man of my dreams,* she'd written inside. Had he given one to her?

The man opens his boot, removes some kind of tool. Get out, he's shouting. At least, that's what Tomasz assumes he's shouting. He can't actually hear since – somehow – the radio volume has increased. 'Lady in Red' plays out loud.

Tomasz's hands remain on the steering wheel. How strange. To be thinking of Lena in a moment like this. How surreal. He pictures her in the crimson bridesmaid dress she wore for her sister's wedding. She hated that dress, said it made her look like a heavy period.

The man pulls at the handle of Tomasz's door.

A heavy period! Tomasz was disgusted at the time. He didn't disagree or tell her she looked good.

The man bangs Tomasz's window. First with his fist, then with the tool.

He didn't tell her she looked good, though now he sees she was beautiful.

Glass shatters into Tomasz's lap. How strange it looks. Surreal. Almost like confetti.

Remi Skytterstad

[No Audible Dialogue]

The commotion and clamour of the airport is deafening. We are turned to lip-readers by the pack of people and their cacophonic humming composed and orchestrated by a medley of *goodbyes / stay safes / I love yous.*

Like a ray of sunshine through a patchy carpet of clouds, is our attention drawn to a

child / boy / son. The crowd of the airport manoeuvring around him—a crop circle of bodies—in unobtrusive / comfortable / safe distances.

The child is fighting tears. His bottom lip quivers, and it's apparent he's trying to be

brave / strong / *a big boy.*

He is embraced by a man / soldier / father. Together they ripple like a wave when he breathes in his son's hair, to treasure / remember / survive. And for a moment time slows inside their circle. The crowds bend past them like light around a black hole—a time lapse of bodies, around their sculpturesque scene. The quivering lips—now still—are stretched from cheek to cheek, in a frozen, soundless cry, revealing gritted milky teeth.

Like this we watch them, as the crowds pour and murmur around them, like a river around an islet.

A woman breaks their event horizon, and the boy and the man come alive again.

The son is nodding to the movement of the father's lips. He straightens his back and wipes away the tears that forced themselves through—his skin darkened in their wake. He moves his mouth in *whys / do you have tos / please don'ts.*

When the man / soldier stands, he leaves—like the shed skin of a snake—the father around the neck of the son. A translucent outline of a man, only hinting at who used to hold the boy.

The boy is embraced by a woman / mother / widow.

Emily Harrison

Not Now, Universe

I tell her about a guy who took me round the back of a fancy Soho restaurant once, to show me the lobsters in the tank holding claws. We are baffled by what men bother to plan for. I tell her I saw him again, weeks later, hanging around my favourite painting in The National Gallery. We laugh at the possibility that he'd been there all day. Maybe other days. I tell her what I was wearing. She nods slowly as she recalls the dress, brings her fingers to her mouth for a chef's kiss. I tell her his flat was higher up than I expected, which was annoying because it meant running down dozens of flights of stairs. She does not interrupt me because she knows where the story is headed. She winces when I tell her how he ripped my underwear off me by forcibly pulling them upwards. Amongst other things. It feels good to give her the details. I tell her how I walked home in the pissing rain, went past two separate karaoke bars where I could hear people murdering Hopelessly Devoted to You. How just before I got home, a man almost hit me with his car and then blew me a kiss. I tell her about this guy posting my underwear back to me a week later, and I'm crying in her arms before we can begin to discuss what a gesture as bold as that could possibly even mean.

Stephanie Carty

The Price of Gingerbread

My brother Hansel went missing. Father frowned into whisky. His wife rubbed kohl down her cheeks before posting selfies on Facebook.

Hansel said he'd spied a shack with walls made from bottles of cherry vodka in the marshlands. He liked to get high on hope. He'd have made a great spaniel, yapping about on the daily walk as if it might be different one time, as if paths weren't already mapped out to always end in the same place.

But a twin is only a twin with a twin.

Through the squelch of mud, I tracked his route. The shack was set back in some trees. Columns of cigarette packets created beams to hold the structure upright. I could have sprinkled those white sticks along the path I'd walked but what was the point when nobody would search for us? Glass bottles arched across the roof. Leeching out of the place was a scent far heavier than father's shirts, woody and dark. I sniffed until the sky spun.

Lights blinked around the door in green and red. I dug my fingers into a crevice to ease out a mobile phone but didn't know the passcode.

After that, it's hazy. Hansel and I were back together yet hardly there at all. There were fiery drinks poured straight from the rafters, sherbet to rub on our gums, pastilles that turned day to night. We giggled like the toddlers we'd been before father's eyes were glazed by grief.

We're not alone here but let's not spoil the tale. Let's not sour the sweet with flashbacks. None of it matters: the strangers, the pressing, the pain. We have the house and the house has us.

My brother reaches out to squeeze my hand. Then we turn to the walls and gorge ourselves.

Alison Powell

Our fathers, who we have strewn like seaweed behind us

We buried our fathers to their necks at Llangennith Beach, at Swanage Bay, at Portreath. They are still there now in their thousands, their balding heads all facing out towards the sea, a hint of something like confusion in their arched eyebrow smiles. They loll and bob their chins against the razor shells, make half-assed jokes about the crabs.

The castles that they built for us have long ago been washed away. And, in the manner of the waves, we have forgotten everything: the kites they flew into the sun, the way they held our arms and lifted us above the surf, the way they gently towel-rubbed our skin.

From our viewpoint in the dunes, we moan in unison, an outburst of lament that grieves across the sky. It is no use. For way too long we've held our fathers out of reach. Afraid of what might foam out from their mouths. Afraid of salty tongues, of scratchy cheeks.

We've lost the tools to raise them from their sandy graves.

And anyway, it's too late now.

The tide is coming in.

Jim Toal

The reallocation of a child's atoms

On board the early morning bus to her cleaning job at the Museo del Prado Fatima reads a magazine article explaining how atoms in a human body are replaced every ten years. Because atoms are neither created nor destroyed it's their redistribution that shapes us into several people in a lifetime.

At work she buffs, mops, and vacuums but isn't allowed to touch the artwork. Her mop swishes past crucifixions and martyrdoms. Her vacuum-cleaner wails at Titian's gruesome depiction of tortured Tityus. Even gentle still-lives are pregnant with loss: the sweet, seeded fruits of her homeland, flowers soft as baby skin.

The last room to clean houses Goya's Black Paintings.

Silencing her vacuum-cleaner, she gawps at raving, moon-eyed Saturn, devouring the headless body of his son. Two skeletal men slobbering over soup, unable to satisfy their appetites. A baying guitarist serenading huddled pilgrims on an unending journey into a gloomy void.

Eventually, she comes to a picture called The Drowning Dog, which captures the last moments of a small dog sinking in what resembles quicksand. With only its head left to be consumed, it looks at Fatima with such perplexed loyalty, such pleading faith, she yearns to reach into the painting, grab it by the scruff and heave it to safety.

For the rest of her shift the image of the hapless dog stays with her. It follows her on the bus journey home. In her tiny flat it sniffs about, wagging its tail. It sits, ears pricked, as she kneels to her prayers. When she picks it up, and it snuggles its damp snout under her armpit, she lullabies a vow. That she'll cling to the hope of liberated atoms and their boundless capacity to conceive new life. It's all she can do to stop herself from slipping under.

Katherine Richards

Air Resistance And Other Forces

Libby hasn't always been a hooker; she learnt Yiddish from her dad, the Torah from her Rabbi, how to braid Challah from her mom.

Libby hasn't always been a hooker, she became one when she dropped out of school and decided she liked sex more than pouring coffee for ungrateful business men in six hundred dollar shoes. *Smile honey, it suits you,* they drawled. *Fuck you,* she mouthed behind their backs. So she quit and now she says her prayers, separates her meat and cheese at dinner before she gets ready for her evening, washing slowly, perfuming gently.

Libby hasn't always been a hooker who knows the pulse of the intersections, the course of the alleys, the vibrations of the city. She woke up with bruises like bracelets once, twice, three times and felt so small, so insignificant that she memorized the streets that led her away through Coal Harbour away to her car in the parkade off Granville away through Gastown away, away. Now she knows each backstreet, cut-through, and park she passes as she leads the men into the dark, into the hotel, motel, boardroom where she pushes them down, straddles, kisses with tongue. Then she retreats, undoes her coat, lets it drop so she's in stilettos and lingerie, garters. These, too, she discards before she saunters forward.

Libby hasn't always been a hooker who enjoys the game; how to catch them, carry them, keep them, but she is now.

She watches for the moment they become hers, the dull gleam that proves she's smarter than them, their letters—MBA, CEO, CFO—made useless.

Libby hasn't always been a hooker who keeps a gun under the pillow.

Andrea Marcusa

The Wait

Let's say you don't call him but wait for his ring like he promised. His words were so genuine when he kissed you goodbye, the way he used to, back when you were together, back when you lived in harmony. "I'll check in tomorrow," he'd said and then let himself out of your home at 3 am.

Let's say by 11 am, you wait outside on the porch. And as you wait to hear his voice again—and the way he makes you laugh— you watch the two goldfish swim round and round in their glass bowl, tails flashing like false promises.

Let's say you wait the whole day. Longer than you ever have before calling. But you don't hear from him. Let's say on the second day you switch off your phone, rest your chin on your hands and let your eyes follow the fish, round and round, unblinking, silent. The refrigerator hums. The traffic outside slows down, stops for the light, then starts up again. Slow. Stop. Start. Over and over, round and round. And still you wait. It grows cold out on the balcony where you sit, but you don't care.

Let's say you switch on your phone and search for a text, a missed call, a voicemail, a tweet. But there's only the sound of traffic. Slow, start, stop. The fish swim.

Let's say you stop yourself each time your mind wanders back to him. His finger sliding down your shoulder blade, his laugh chiming in you like a church bell. The heat of his chest as his arms surround you. Instead you press your chin hard into your hands until it hurts.

Let's say you drag the vacuum across the floor, it's motor moaning as it whirrs. You scrub the toilet with a brush, you finally make your bed. When you're finished, you look up and see the rain begin. You take a seat back on the balcony and ignore the small bird pecking at the floor, or see the creature pause, stare straight at you and cock its head like a question. Let's say you barely notice the sky clear, the salmon heavens, the lilac clouds and evening star as the sun sinks. The bird pecks some more, flies up and lands on the fishbowl, then springs into the night sky and flies away. And still you keep your chin pressing in, your body still. Only the fish keep moving, round and round. Going in circles.

Catherine Ogston

How It Ends

"What you need," says Anna, "is a woman's touch." You watch her pull elegantly shaped mugs from a bag, their labels swinging in the draught. Then she hangs a new oven glove by the cooker and places a loaf with seeds you can't identify in the breadbin.

The next day she examines some cushions and you see with new eyes that the cream fabric has turned to dirty beige. Climbing into the island car with the broken window, you notice the detritus littering the floor and a dried-up crab shell on the dashboard. "Sorry," you say and she smiles a half-smile back.

Later you walk up the hill behind the house, mottled grey cloud covering the postcard-perfect sea views. Over the ridge, a sheep runs in frantic zig-zags making the two of you stop and stare. Her lambs are dead. The ewe staggers, pleading with desperate bleats for help but the twin lambs are huddled together, their thin bodies sinking into the grass.

"Can't you do something?" says Anna and you shrug because there is nothing to be done. You leave the small ruined creatures there, their mother still making hopeful circuits, back and forth, her heavy udder swinging.

She is quiet all evening and you pretend to fall asleep in the heat of the fire. She goes upstairs first. You brush your teeth knowing that, in bed, your fingertips will touch her shoulder, barrier-stiff, and she will say nothing but roll to the mattress edge. In the morning she will announce she is going back to the city and you will stand on the pier and wave goodbye, while planning on a day of whatever you fancy and some whisky that night, the new oven glove burning brightly in the woodburner and the loaf scattered for the birds.

Sara Hills

Pill Babies

My brother Benny dares me to eat my babies. He promises me a dollar for each one. I don't want to eat them, but I tell him seven dollars would buy me a plastic doll like the other girls have. One that pees and bats her eyes.

I remove the damp log and place the woodlice in my palm. Their bodies roly-poly into little pills.

"Shhh," I say, sounding just like Mama. "No one's gonna hurt you."

I open my mouth and drop one in quick. Real quick for a real baby. It curls up on my tongue and I swear I hear it crying. It pops between my teeth, like wax-covered candy. Only dirt-flavored.

Benny cackles, mouth wide, squealing like a rusty hinge. His molars are dark, packed in chocolate. Chocolate he didn't share with me.

I gag and spit the mangled baby into the dirt.

"Not like this," I say.

We take the babies into the kitchen and heat a slice of butter in a pan. When it's yellowy good and sizzling, I squinch my face and let one fall. It pills when it hits the heat, snaps, then relaxes open. We sauté them, one by one, and spread them on a plate.

"D-d-dig in," Benny says. The whatchamacallit on his neck bobs up and down, like he's swallowing for me.

Benny doesn't have seven dollars, and we both know it. The only baby we'll get is the one Mama's cooking in her belly from Mr. Ryarson. The baby that caused Daddy to drink a bottle of whiskey, call Benny the r-word, and hold Benny's ear to the hot stove.

"Are you ready?" I ask.

Benny's eyes light into a grin. He squeals and claps joyously, as I take the first bite.

Michelle Elvy

Roll the die

THREE. Past present future. Which path, eh? Past is dead. Never mind Faulkner. Present: a maze. Future: Don't go there. Roll again, boy.

SIX. Count the days since you spoke. Draw a line in the sand. Stay still: stop where you are. Don't talk don't listen don't blink. Don't break don't breathe don't think. Throw the die once more and…

ONE. Easy. Stop. Broken. Repair? Listen. Sleep. Again.

FIVE. Can't sit still, not now. Slipping, sleeping, in and out. This moment, a fleeting free-for-all. A dream-state spinning roulette table. Black-red-black-red-black. Five words in a promise. *I will never leave you*. You thought *Never say never*. But you didn't say it.

FOUR. You blow for luck. Which works, it seems…

   – 'cause this time you're down on the Wannsee, wading in the shallows, sister grinning goofy, Mum laying out the picnic. Dad's there untangling the rigging on your model sailboat. He'll make it work this time. He always makes it work. You are happy you are happy you are happy – again. The past is dead but it's a good dream still and –

Wake up, roll again. Dreams aren't really real. This is: game's ending. Hold on, hold it. Squeeze the die, squint. Roll it, believe it.

Two. Morning light. Sticky thoughts. And him.

> Pocket him. Shoot him. *Fuck him*. Consume him.
> Hum him. Sing him. Burn him. Love him.
> Forget him. Forever him.

Wake up.

Claire Hart

The Weight Of A Heart

Luca carries his boy up to bed when he falls asleep in the car. He treads carefully on the stairs, his wife breezing ahead, opening doors and pulling down covers. She steps back, allowing Luca to pass. *You've smoothed out all the creases again*, he says, laying his boy down—first hips, then feet, then head.

They've been at the beach all day and Luca's skin feels warm and tight. There will be sand in this bed, but these things don't matter as they did. He kneels, watching his boy sleeping; mouth open, the soft push and pull of his breath like the waves on the stones.

They swam in the sea today. His wife sat watching even though he told her to lie back and rest. The current pulled at his body when they waded in deeper, his boy's legs wrapped at his waist. Luca saw his wife stand, her hand to her neck. *You're like a big boat, Daddy*, his boy said as Luca swam them back to the shore.

There is a ticking clock on the bedroom wall. Like your heart, Daddy, his boy always says. Luca counts out the beats. The doctors repaired his aneurysm as best they could. *The aorta is the main road out of the heart*, one said, *there's been a lot of traffic, at your age.*

He used to be the village strong man, before he watched time.

Luca has taken to kissing his son on an in-breath, drinking in his sweet, salty skin—not wanting to waste a second or spill a drop. The four chambers of his heart expand with these surges of emotion, absorbing it all like a sponge soaks up water—his heart so heavy—full of love so light.

Gail Anderson

The Wishbone House

His bones are fifteenth-century, his lungs two great rooms filled with Welsh wind. He stands in the field, watches his house. Cruck framed, sinewed with reed and daub, held aloft by a mighty oak, cleft. Two equal curves, spread feet planted in earth, heads joined at the peak.

Each night, in sleep, it is spring. Primrose and poppy, the sky darted with starlings. What year it is he cannot tell, and does not care. All he knows is that she is there, her kirtle tied above strong calves, her fine hair caught in a linen caul. They walk an undulation of ridge-and-furrow fields, scything side by side. Spelt and barley, flax bearded with strawberry. In this sleeping world their house is young, its timbers supple, plaster true. Evenings, logs tumble to hearth. The rooms yawn, fragrant with wild herbs. Her block-printed curtains breathe from the casements. The oak soars over their heads, an up-ended heart.

Each morning he jolts to cold consciousness, the warmth of her pressed hands fading on his chest, his hounds nosing and chuffing for something lost beneath the floorboards.

Waking, it is winter, and the house is old. The roof moans and shifts. Slates fall into the yard, walls fissure and weep. He closes room after room, leaves them to the mice and bats. Try as he like, the fire won't warm him.

He must leave this place, he knows. Hitch out between cord-swung gates and not look back. Far away, church bells beckon, an ululation in freshening air.

But he stays, clag-footed, deep rooted. His bones are fifteenth-century, his heart beats back the years. He hears a call to higher ground.

Evie Prichard

The Dinosaur

Mama calls Daddy a dinosaur. You ask him what that means, after the shouting is over.

Dinosaurs, he tells you, are old. Older even than he is.

They're scaly, like the lizards that flicker over your balcony tiles faster than shooting stars.

Only dinosaurs are big lizards, sloooooow lizards.

You laugh at his face saying that word, how his wrinkles rearrange themselves and his barely-there lips look like a kiss.

Later – "Careful, habibi, Daddy's back isn't what it was," – you trundle through ancient swamps, sulphur belching sharp into the air. A T-Rex eyes you from behind a clump of ferns: Daddy is hardly fast enough to save you. Giggle-screaming, eye-streaming, you ask – when will I see a real dinosaur?

Daddy's laughter huffs to a stop.

"My darling, I'm so sorry. The dinosaurs died, long, long ago."

"How?"

"An asteroid…A shooting star. It hit the earth and it burned everything."

You nod, giggles deserting you. You understand.

He looks at you, and he smiles an odd smile. "Here, come here, habibi. Look out the window with me."

In the street a flock of small birds scatters like smoky breath on the breeze. A crow claims a telephone wire high above the sun-scorched pavement.

"The birds were dinosaurs once, habibi. Now look at them."

You follow a finch with your eyes, and you smile.

That evening, the stars fall again. The ground shakes with them.

You curl into Daddy in the cellar, dreaming about dinosaurs as he and Mama argue.

"There are other universities, other lives for us!" she hisses.

He doesn't answer.

Into the silence, you ask something that's been pecking at you all day.

"Daddy, how did the birds survive the shooting star?"

Daddy squeezes you tighter. "They flew away, habibi."

He takes Mama's hand, and nods.

"They flew away."

Katie Oliver

The Butcher

Sam's boss, Archie, was in the war and doesn't let anyone forget it. He punctuates tales of slaughter in faraway lands with the whistle of cold metal and the thunk of raw meat. Chunks of bloody debris splatter across the counter while Sam tries to concentrate upon the rosemary centrepiece he is making for the window display.

Archie killed a guy once. He likes to act it out using the carcass of whichever hapless creature he's carving at the time; the chopping always becomes especially frenzied during this particular anecdote. Sam discreetly removes a piece of flyaway gristle from his cheek, and says: *Yes boss*.

He busies himself with trimming the racks of lamb, working with deft precision. Archie has been grudgingly impressed by the speed at which he has mastered this most intricate of tasks. *Delicate hands*, he sniffs. *S'pose someone needs 'em.*

Archie's hands are large and coarse, the fine lines on his palms a grisly network of old gore. At the end of each shift, Sam soaks his own hands in lemon juice, and launders his apron with a double dose of fabric softener. At mealtimes, he eats his vegetables but slides the meat to the side of his plate. Privately, he starts experimenting with lentils.

At night, Sam tries to rid himself of the image of Archie hacking a young man to death. He thinks about the application form hidden at the bottom of his wardrobe, and dreams of warm, living bodies draped in beautiful fabric.

Giles Montgomery

Jigsaw Puzzle Piece

You know that thing you do with a jigsaw puzzle piece when you've been working on a particular spot for ages and you've tried so many pieces and some of them were almost right but not quite and some were so wrong that you actually laughed at yourself for even thinking they would fit and eventually – just when you're done with this stupid jigsaw and jigsaws in general for that matter, like who even cares? – you try one last piece and it slots into place so effortlessly that your fingers don't know what to do with themselves so you give the piece a little tap even though it's already perfectly in place but it's more about your need to show how happy you are that the piece came along at the right moment and reaffirmed your belief in jigsaw puzzles? Well, anyway, that's why I tapped you on the head just now.

Dettra Rose

Firebird and The Phoenix

Dirty scarlet sky. Burnt copper sun. Greedy orange flames, soaring black plumes. Trees snapping, falling. Flung our cat and old photos in the car. Fled.

Next day. Pale ash on the ground like dead snow. Turned rubble over, searching for ourselves in lives already cremated. Firebird, nature's thief, stole everything.

Parked a beat-up silver caravan where the house burned, the two of us and the scorched cat moved in. Cat hid when I struck matches to light my smokes, bandages on his paws. My wife went to the relief centre, brought back charity clothes. White rage bellowed out of me and I chucked them in the creek. Two months on, my wife's pork chop arms were sticks and she left carrying an empty suitcase. Tears on my skin.

Neighbours came to my door; smoke stink in their clothes too. Woman with them I know from town, she lost the lot. Stories I recognised spilling in her eyes. Helen, is her name. Neighbours shoved me into the community hall, folks there filling on hot meals and cold beers. Different names but tears the same, folding around each other when they cried. We ate together most nights. Helen played a rosy guitar; voice like water trickling over river stones. Pushed a smile out of me.

Everything is before or after the fires. Time split. People split. Some couldn't leave; others had to go. I've planted eucalypts back in the same spots, means I've survived. But firebird could swoop again anytime. Life. It's tissue paper.

I'm necking beer on the deck, new house proud on the old site. Helen's on the front steps strumming, strumming a new rhythm she's finding words for. Phoenix-like we've risen from ashes, but ghost flames still holler in my ears and I shake lighting the kindling at night.

Johanna Robinson

Backfire

They reckon it was Joey who burned down the long, low shed. Couldn't stand the pop-crack-creak-snap of the stems. Said the noise was like radio crackle, like they were trying to get in touch with him. "Who?" I'd asked him. "Spirits," he said.

I asked him which ones, for we have many here, in our little Yorkshire frost pocket between the hills. Joey never answered.

Us girls did the work when the lads were away. We snapped the rhubarb like spines, our backs aflame. We yearned for the light, same as the crop did. We grew pale as the forced fruit blushed. We were safe, though, in our dark sheds lit by candles, as the planes ploughed the night above us.

When the boys came back, we gave them crumble, spooning it into their mouths. But the fruit was bitter; there was no sugar for the topping, only oats that stuck to their dry lips, and which they could not swallow.

We showed them what to do. We fitted them with our aprons and taught them ancient tricks. Sprinkle the shoots with water to pretend it's spring. Give them heat. Deny them light. I taught Joey how to lever out each stem at its base. I watched his pupils grow large and told myself it wasn't because he was scared.

Pop-crack. He'd flinch and I almost laughed: "It's just the stalks. They groan as they grow."

Pop-crack. "Everything sounds loud in silence, in the dark," he said.

The shed caught easily, its floor bedded with wool from the mills to keep the crop warm. The roots gave up like tinder. The air smelled of blackened sugar. The shed burned so brightly, as we watched, that our pupils turned to pins and the flames danced in our eyes: red, yellow, crackling.

Rebecca Tantony

The Birch Tree

I decided on a neon green bikini that ties at the sides. I knew I was probably too much flesh for such a thing, but we were 178 miles from home so I convinced myself of wearing it. Before we left, I fake tanned my entire body a subtle orange.

It had been the same holiday every year. A rotation of various women cooking meals, my brother and I fighting for attention, me climbing on the bench to sing the latest chart hits, him pulling his pants down in the middle of a restaurant.

What I remember most is the pond and the gang of bullrushes around it. I remember the older girls who were staying in a barn near ours, how they would smoke by the mouth of the water, then throw their cigarette ends in. They seemed so self-assured, mouths pink and red, all belly tops and protruding rib bones. Every time they swore I would blink as if something harsh had been flicked into my eye. Then watch how they plaited their hair, leant on each others shoulders, or never faltered in letting another girl know they were so much more than their recent heartbreak.

I had a holiday romance, but he came and he left. It was the girls who went everywhere with me from there on in. Or some version of them anyway. No matter what happens, the years that unravel, the men that arrive and leave, those girls remain.

I ask them if they can help me find what was once mine and they take me to a birch tree. With nicotine hands they carve my initials into the trunk and tell me this: without a boy above it or a heart between you both, life is a journey back to your name.

Hannah Storm

Sarajevo Rose

Damir buys a bouquet once a month at Chelsea market. Seven long-stemmed roses. Always red. He hands the flowerseller ten bucks, watches her count the change into his palm – nickels, quarters, pennies.

Now he can tell the coins apart, but there was a time he couldn't. He remembers that first day when the change slipped from his grasp, ricocheting like shrapnel. They both ducked to the cobbles, rising together so he could not resist her gaze.

"They say life spins on a dime," she said, returning the smallest silver. He nodded, but all he understood was that her eyes were blue like a Sarajevo summer sky, and when she said 'dime', it sounded like his name.

Back home, 'Damir' meant peace. Here it meant scorn, it meant stranger, it meant the soiled sheets of a bedsit he could scarcely afford, in a building shaken by each passing train.

The roses stand in a soda bottle on the window ledge. His only luxury – even the bottle was borrowed from the bum downstairs. Damir never considers going without them, and when winter comes, he wears all his clothes to reduce the bills so he can still visit the market.

On his way to the flowerseller, he remembers a day in Markhale with his sister, her hand slippery with a seven-year-old's excitement. The hills around Sarajevo had been quiet. He remembers a young woman dropping a single, precious coin. Damir ducked to retrieve it. She did too. He remembers her sky-blue eyes. He doesn't remember dropping his sister's hand.

The building shook with the blast. When he looked up, his sister was gone. Damir has read how Sarajevans painted red roses in the shell's concrete scars. When his flowers wilt, the petals fall to the floor. Damir never picks them up.

Elena Croitoru

Daughter

Two months before I crossed the border, my father and I went to the only church left in Deir ez-Zor. The place was covered in burns, its pillars were peeling off as if some sort of disease was spreading from us to our buildings. I held my father's elbow as we climbed the makeshift steps. Our feet sank periodically into the debris because underneath the fragments of baby bathtubs, singed shirts and bent teaspoons, there were the remains of those the government couldn't dig out.

Inside, the air was heavy with cement powder which lined our windpipes and lungs as we spoke, turning us into statues covered in skin. A barn swallow flew in through a cross-shaped window. My father took out sunflower seeds from his pocket, then scattered them on the floor, stumbling because he wasn't yet used to his prosthetic leg, which One Nation had donated the previous week.

We sat down, but my father struggled to keep his balance as the feet of our plastic chairs were uneven. By the arched altar, the wooden Jesus was bullet-ridden, and I kept thinking that our world was disappearing, hole by hole.

When the sermon started, we all looked as if we weren't quite there. I scratched the bumpy scar on my cheek, the place where my soul must have escaped. It must have done because it was no longer inside me or maybe the soul is just something we talk about but stop believing in. My father listened despite being almost deaf. I wanted to tell him that I'd decided to leave our country for good.

When the swallow hopped by his foot, pecking at the crumbled cement, he said, "Remind me to bring more seeds next time."

I opened my mouth and said nothing.

Johanna Robinson

[Insert title here], a novel

CHAPTER ONE

In which our protagonist is born to a mother cursing a blue streak, the pressure of forceps stained on her forehead, her large hands clasping out and eyes crushed shut.

CHAPTER TWO

In which our protagonist learns the playground rules until the rules are bent and words are twisted, and no one tells tales and it's not so much fun to skip alone.

CHAPTER THREE

In which our heroine becomes a woman but feels a girl and in the bath scrubs her legs with pumice to rid them of hair because there are never, ever razors in the house.

CHAPTER FOUR

In which a pill is taken to flush out something as there's only room for one protagonist at this stage of the story.

CHAPTER FIVE

In which our heroine dreams she's a magpie standing on her little-girl dressing table among lipsticks stolen and never worn and in which our magpie preens in the mirror, feeling like *one* but seeing *two*.

CHAPTER SIX

In which years have passed and we meet our protagonist again, and in which when we turn the page, we are reminded of how she turns back the blanket on her bed, over and over.

CHAPTER SEVEN

In which our protagonist finds herself in hospital holding a water-born baby that looks at her as though she knows everything about her.

CHAPTER EIGHT

In which our girl, our woman, our mother, our daughter, struggles to navigate when doubt bobs like a string of buoys and the saltwater still stings.

CHAPTER NINE

In which they swim.

CHAPTER TEN

In which our heroine sets sail with her daughter the skipper; in which one protagonist says there are no footsteps to follow on the ocean, which never, ever ends.

Anika Carpenter

Loosened Objects

The flowers, lace-fine dashes of white glaze, on Nurse Hughes' mug of steaming coffee are going melt and drip onto the carpet, leaving a wet patch for someone to take the blame for. I need to say it, and I can, so I do, "We should be drinking from cups painted to look like wells, with bright pink handles the shape of S's. Why not let us hold in our hands the thought of fresh water and feeling good?"

The Duty Manager rounds the corner, slaps a regularly moisturised hand against the plastic cover of her clipboard. The unsound smack knocks Nurse Hughes' thoughtful answer right out of her head and onto the floor with the pool of lost blooms.

"This is your final warning, Hughes, Ms Russell is not your friend, your job here is to ensure she is safe, not to add to her confusion."

A warden comes, steers me back to the dayroom. It holds in lungfuls of stale air and a semi-circle of high-backed chairs staring down a wall-mounted television tuned to a shopping channel. A woman with a short, sharp bob is demonstrating decoupage. She lays out and glues down cherubs and bunches of roses. "My love," I scold the TV, "is unstuck, it bounds from person to person happy as a puppy." Angie, a fifty-five-year-old sales executive whose chest feels like 'an overweight doped-up house cat,' reaches for me, "I need some air."

I try to sound as much as possible like I'm never any trouble and ask, "May we go into the garden, please?"

The warden smokes while Angie and I walk circuits looking for loosened objects; tulip petals, feathers, magnolia leaves, hairpins. We decipher their landed patterns as instructions for dance steps; gliding from object to object makes us feel better.

Shannon Savvas

Chicken Fat

Sundays are Maisie's come to God (or whatever you want to call it) days. She roasts two chooks, fragrant with thyme and bay, no garlic.

"Tick tock every time," Ewan says, "Nothing like a good roast chicken."

Maisie agrees.

Later, she shreds the leftovers for sandwiches, pâté and pies stuffed with leeks and bacon through the week and boils the carcass, strains the slippery gorgeousness leeched from its bones through muslin into a bowl to cool and thicken. Come evening, she ladles the chicken jelly into a jar for soups, casseroles and frying vegetables. She also fills the small frosted-glass jar she keeps in her bedside drawer, once filled with Anti-Aging Face Cream (well that never worked) but which now sparks joy, as that sheng fui mumbo jumbo woman says on the telly.

Maisie remembers her mother sitting each evening by the fire, massaging her heels and hands. Her mother's hands were beautifully soft and always smelt of a chicken roast dinner.

Maisie also has soft hands. She rubs the unctuous schmaltz, not downstairs with her menfolk watching the weekend sports on cable but upstairs in the locked bathroom with the contents of the package she had delivered to Erin O'Connor's place in the village. She'd told Erin it was a birthday surprise for Ewan. She couldn't risk having it delivered to the farm where neither husband or boys recognised the sanctity of the post and named addressee.

Now on Sunday nights, Maisie has found places her mother never thought of to rub the golden gel, new ways of finding pleasure, new ways to keep going through the long hot summers and snowed in winters on the farm with a man who fucks like a pig and three boys who never stop eating.

Luckily, they love chicken.

Vance Cariaga

The Whole Bird

First wait for the tap on the shoulder, then breathe deep. Slide your hand to the zipper and yank it quick like. Open the pocket wide, wide enough for a football, wide enough so he can drop a chicken inside before you zip it back up.

Always a whole chicken, never parts. Can't trust parts of a chicken, he told me. Can't trust the butcher, can't trust the meat, maybe one part came from a righteous bird and one from a trifling bird and six from a bird should've been ground into cat food.

Stand in his shadow, backpack down low, away from roving eyes. Don't give yourself away. Don't get that guilty look. Breathe deep, you're just a kid with a backpack.

Side pouches are for small items. An onion, chips, a can of beer.

Can't cook without an onion, he said.

Can't eat without cooking.

Can't buy decent food with no job.

Can't find no jobs worth having.

He told me: Life lays out certain expectations. You got to expect the best or you get the parts instead of the whole bird. One day he'll find work again, real soon. But not just any job. Got to be the right job. The whole bird.

Meantime, we got to eat, right?

We have a plan in case I get caught. He'll grab me, yank my head up, tell me he didn't raise no ungodly child, loud like, for all the right ears. Then tell the store manager, Can you believe this wayward young 'un?

But we never been caught, not yet.

He told me: They let kids slide, but not no grown-ass man.

When we get home he tells Mama to cook that bird up right.

I go sit outside, alone, breathing deep.

María Alejandra Barrios Vélez

Apagón 1992

The blackout starts after eight and when we walk in the neighborhood it feels like it's ready to betray us. Tonight after dinner with Abuela, I walk the streets with Luis so we can say goodbye before he goes to the deep forest. Abuela and Luis are all I have left to protect me. This country with all its darkness will suffocate all the boys that make it out to the forest. I am a woman so I don't suffocate. I wait. For men to come back, for the morning so I can make the arepas. For light.

After the military groups recruit in the neighborhood, Luis can't talk about anything else. "It's my turn," he says and I try to memorize the lines in his face, the softness of his cheeks and his musky smell. Luis is going to make of his mom a woman without purpose and he doesn't care. In the darkness, I can see him practicing how to hold a fusil like the ones the guerrilleros carry when they visit us. Like the ones they lean towards us when they want us to cook.

"Papá didn't have fight in him but I do," he says. Scared that someone will hear us, I kiss him so he shuts up.

The next night, I stand outside alone like a man and I open my hands like a little nest and close my eyes. Luis has left me with nothing but a small fire I can start with the palms of my hands. By now, he must be reaching the forest.

The fire burns so strongly that if I chose to, I could start a bigger one of my own.

Christopher Allen

How We Eat

This is us: Mom going on about the godless world, Dad watching for the Viet Cong in the backyard trees, when Brandon looks up from his overcooked broccoli and says, "You ever heard the earth breathe?"

"Plants breathe," Mom says, "and volcanoes sure do exhale sometimes."

"Know what I mean?" Brandon says to Dad—loud like he thinks it'll wake him.

He means Jilliane. *When Jilliane looks my way. When Jilliane flies away. The Earth breathes.* While he burns burgers at Hardee's, I pick his lock, search his journal for clues in his songs that he killed her.

"Have they found that girl?" I ask. Jilliane's been missing three days.

"You know what they say," Mom says to Dad.

We know. She's said it enough. After 72 hours, all you'll find is a body, bloated and covered with leaves. I know Brandon did it. He's possessed. But he's not a bad songwriter.

Dad slaps the table, goes over to the window. "You feed the rabbits?" He's a sergeant barking at shadows of soldiers out there in the trees. I always feed the rabbits. I'm not a shadow, I want to say. I'm not a soldier.

"I mean," Brandon says, "the feeling when you come undone. Like you had something, and now you don't." He turns to Dad, back at the table now panting. "You know that feeling?"

But Dad's shoving broccoli into his mouth like if he doesn't strike camp now, we will all explode.

Gillian O'Shaughnessy

How to Light a Coal Fire

Coal is hard to work with when you didn't grow up with it. It's like trying to burn stone. And the fire's out. Again. I kneel in the early morning remnants of my last effort and begin a silent routine. The grate must be clean, so first the ash-pan is emptied and swept. I take more than my allotted ration of firelighters from their box, at least six, and arrange them in a small circle. Then construct a tower of pine-chip kindling leaving plenty of gaps for air flow.

I stop to check on you. Asleep, thank god, a tiny bird in a pillow nest to help you breathe. The air's thick with morphine. Your hand is raised and slightly bent, as though you still grip a cigarette and all my failures are scattered down the front of your red robe like grim black polka dots on a party dress. I make my way quietly back to the fireside, listening for the chink of your lighter to tell me you're awake. I'm always listening.

I take small lumps of coal from the bucket, lay them carefully among the fire bed then find the matches hidden from you earlier and strike one. The noise makes me wince. Three more tries, then at last it catches.

Later, you shuffle in to check on my work on your way to the couch. *How many firelighters* –you ask. *Just one* – I lie. A statue of Mary on the mantelpiece forgives me, with rapt expression and arms benevolently outstretched. When your brothers arrive for breakfast, they kiss you gently so as not to hurt you and you hold court in your crimson gown, your face glowing from the warmth of my coal fire.

Stephen J Vowles

Swings & Roundabouts

I have brought my woman home for Christmas, our first together. The house is warm and full of comforting smells. Lunch is not far away.

My father shuffles into the lounge, he is sheepish and his cheeks are flushed.

"She's walked out."

"What?"

"Your mother," his lips move but he stumbles upon the other words.

I check the garage, the car inside. I walk not knowing where to look, what to do. Then I remember the park, the playground; happy times.

Away from the house it doesn't feel festive.

I find her sitting on the merry go round. She has set it in gentle motion and once I have made up the distance between us, I climb aboard.

We glide silently around and around.

"I'm not coming back, he can't take his gin, he never could."

She returns to her thoughts and I wonder about their life together.

From the tree-line a crow rattles and caws.

"Your brother used to make himself completely giddy on this thing." Then as an after thought she says, "And you were a bloody menace on those swings."

I smile fondly, not for myself, but because it is what is required.

"Yeah, he always was a self destructive little sod."

There is a sudden chill breeze and the dried carcasses of dead leaves scrape across the cold black tarmacadam.

We come to a standstill, the moment has passed.

She stands up, resolve stiffening her back.

"What must that lovely girl of yours be thinking? Fine example, I am, and her growing up without a mother and all."

When we get back, my father meets us at the door.

"I've turned up the spuds for the last charge and the turkey is rested. Shall I get on and carve?"

Michelle North-Coombes

Dust

On a January day, they fish his body from the river and lay him down on a plastic sheet alongside many others.

Our cousin, Mahmoud, sends me a video of him lying there, hands tied behind his back, tape stretched across his mouth. His eyes are wide open as if surprised by the bullet-hole through his head. Above the shouts of grief, I hear helicopters circling overhead and picture them silhouetted against the sun like predatory insects.

As boys, we ran through my grandfather's pistachio orchards, chased fat-tailed Awassi sheep through rocky fields. Every autumn, my grandmother would rise early to harvest the Damask roses before the sun stole their scent. I smelt them when she bent to kiss my forehead. "Each rose has 30 petals," she said. "Each one."

This morning, Nasir and I are in Oxford, fitting stone benchtops in a kitchen. The owner lets us in through the back door and offers us tea or coffee. We avert our eyes and tell her it is Ramadan. She looks bemused and heads back upstairs.

We get to work. It's a big job for two men. My brother had hoped to join us by now. He was a merchant but willing to adapt to something new. It is cold outside but we still sweat as we cut the heavy slabs. The dust flies up and coats us until we look like ghosts in white shrouds.

Tonight, I'll rinse the dust from my body, the grit from my eyes which are now the same colour as the pomegranate juice that ran down our chins when we were boys. The same colour that ran from the wound in my brother's temple when they shot him.

He would have been 30 today. One of the oldest men they found in that river.

Kate Lee

How I summoned a monster

It was an enchantment made me do it. I watched as my hand reached for the tennis ball, scooped it from its earthy nest beneath the laurel leaves. I gripped it so hard my knuckles shone like white pebbles. I licked my winter lips, tongue lingering on each painful groove, while my fingers stroked the ball's damp velvet surface and traced its rubber rivers. Still hard as stone, despite its hibernation. The robin on the fence, round red guard, hopped away.

It was time.

I climbed onto the upturned wheelbarrow and balanced like a king. Raising my arm in a glorious arc, I sent the fluffy green ammunition flying fast and fearless into enemy territory. High copper hedges laced with frost stood sentry in front of the monster's greenhouse, but my aim was true. The glass exploded, the sound echoing across the lawns like shocked cheers. I jumped down and hid beneath the laurel bush. Curling into a ball, I buried a hot grin in my knees. Blood thudded in my ears.

Mr Ellis-Jones came roaring from the big house and spat dirty words onto his immaculate garden path, step by stamping step, a green-fingered black-hearted white-haired ogre, and it was magical.

Iona Winter

The wife of the tree shaker

Last week I watched a white man shake a tree with such fierceness, that sleeping kakapō fell to the ground like sacks of kūmara. That man had a wife, Mrs Douglas.

I met her this afternoon, on my way to gather kai from the ocean.

She said, "Hello," and thrust out her hand towards me.

For a tiny woman, Mrs Douglas was quick to describe how efficiently she had learned to shoulder her husband's rifle. She gesticulated with hands and arms to make her point.

Putting this skill to good use, she explained how she brought the kererū down 'in a very sportsman-like manner.' And then went on to say how her good friend Alice, who was 'not as accomplished' as she with the gun, was content to 'carry the bag' whenever the two women went shooting.

"Do your people eat the wood pigeon?" she asked.

"Only in winter," I replied, "for there are rules about these things."

"Oh?" she said.

It was not appropriate to tell her why. An uneasy silence presented itself, before she rapidly continued on with her story.

At dusk, Mrs Douglas said she walked 'armed' with an umbrella. For there were numerous bats at that time of day, and they frequently bumped into her.

"The collisions are not a bother," she said.

Mrs Douglas told me how she enjoyed 'the subtle violence' when their silken bodies glanced off her exposed skin. Then she said she wished she could use the rifle on her tāne at night, when he lay in a stupor with his flies loose.

She told me this because she did not think I understood her tongue. But when our eyes met, a realisation surpassed our contrasting skins — such is the shared history of women.

Jayne Morley

Comic Confinement

It was going to be some feat, size fifteen to be frank (audience laughter), living with a clown, particularly during lockdown, and especially as he wasn't funny. He had his moments but there were going to be a lot of those, one hundred and thirty-one thousand, four hundred to be accurate (audience sniggers). And he could fill about ten of those. Minutes that is, not shoes (audience groans). It was worse when he mislaid his red nose, which was often, and spent half an hour debating whether Amazon was appropriate (audience boos), and then another half-hour ordering the best deal (audience applauds knowingly). Then re-ordering when he found one complete with elastic. Having discovered the whereabouts of the missing nose when the parcel arrived, by the time he had found his white gloves and his mask to answer the door, the delivery man would have gone, leaving a note saying "left with neighbour" and as we lived in a flat it took time checking which resident had it. Of course everyone he approached was happy to have a distancing drink with a clown and he would return late, stumbling into the flat having forgotten his reason for leaving (audience roars). I wasn't going to be able to cope with another ninety-three thousand one hundred and fifty further minutes of this nonsense so, in an effort to appease, discovered a Zoom tutor who taught me how to crochet woollen balls in under five minutes (audience cheers). It wasn't long before my creative efforts filled his side of the bed, and I realised that the reason

I had fallen for him – slipped in fact – (audience snigger), was the iconic symbol itself, and spent the rest of my confinement chuckling, in splendid isolation, beneath an eiderdown of the sweetest red noses.

Marissa Hoffmann

Rwanda 1994

When Patricia swept an Albertine owl pellet from her red earth compound, her children were away collecting water. The sticks in her broom tore open the neat grey parcel of mouse fur, cockroach shell fragments, cockroach legs.

"Ay," Patricia said, shaking her head. She smiled into the trees. She knew the owl watched her night and day.

Patricia's neighbour Aloys heard the owl hooting, and he heard his leaders saying, *Fill the graveyards.* And the radio DJ saying, *There are snakes and cockroaches among us.* And he remembered his old teacher told him, *A group of owls is a parliament, a group of cockroaches is an intrusion.*

The owl circled high above the men who hacked at the legs and the arms, who threw the snaky bodies into the river, slippery, bobbing, gliding around rocks, dipping and tumbling. Downstream they were swollen, they were facedown and joined a crowd in Lake Victoria, bumping into each other silently.

The Albertine owl has no ears, but it heard one hundred days of screaming. Its eyes can only look straight, but it witnessed a million dying. It tried not to watch, it turned its head 270 degrees, but it saw who killed Patricia's children, who cut her face with a machete, who broke her shoulder, left her body against a tree, her underwear pulled down.

Today, in the land where God comes to rest on a Sunday, the femurs and the skulls lie unnamed on the shelves in the church, and Patricia and Aloys are neighbours again. They sit at noon on the baked red earth beneath a tree in the marketplace. They listen to the reconciliation trials, and the Albertine owl listens too. And because the truth is too sharp to digest, they've all had to learn to make themselves spit up.

Carol A Stone

Raisin Days

The silent guard beckons Joseph up to the bars, slides the tray beneath the cell door. Joseph obeys, picks up the tray carrying the same unappetising daily ration of gristle, stale bread and water. Today, however, a small dish of raisins sits on the tray. Joseph knows only too well what their appearance means. It is the day of his beating, the day when the other guards drag him from his cell to tether him beneath the cruel sun, to flog him in the hope of breaking him enough to reveal his regiment's military plans and locations. Despite this harrowing realisation the raisins are a welcome distraction, a thoughtful gift the unspeaking guard brings each time a beating is scheduled. Joseph issues a nod of gratitude, a silent promise made to repay the guards' compassion as soon as he is free.

Joseph chews the raisins one by one, churning them over so the sticky sweet taste conceals the bitterness occasionally bursting upon his tongue, careful to dab away any powdery residue from the corners of his mouth with water. Outside he can hear his captors gathering, smells their hashish which drifts up through his barred window. For a while he listens to their conversations spoken in words he cannot understand until those words become distant in the familiar light-headedness which creeps over him. He rests his head against the cool clay wall as the raisins begin to take their intoxicating hold. Soon he will be ready for the guards to do their bidding, his mind too inebriated to be part of the event, his speech too tangled to spill any secrets, his flesh so numb those biting whips will be nothing more than whispers upon his skin.

Hazel Osmond

Full spider

His brothers lay serried in neat rows on the war memorial, but there were no letters outlined in gold for shrapnel wounds. No ceremony with a band.

He got a life limped through. She propped him up – wife, nurse, servant. Absorbed the anger that leaked from his hands into her skin.

Now he can't even make a fist.

She knows every creak of him; listens for the wheeze of his lungs as the leaves yellow. Hates how he sits crouch-backed in front of the television, jabbing the carpet with his stick.

Sometimes he'll lean it, sly-slanted, against furniture. Laugh when she stumbles over it and call her clumsy.

He seems happier when the stick becomes two crutches. Holds them like double sceptres as he issues edicts and commands.

Waiting for the kettle to boil, she looks up to see him peg and swing his way towards her. Four legs are quicker than two; she needs to factor that in.

After he's settled in bed, she decants white wine into herself and imagines bringing those metal sticks down on his skull. Using the prison bars to break free.

They battle on.

One afternoon, he misjudges the front step and pirouettes into the hydrangea bush.

"No major harm," the doctor says. "But, perhaps …"

A young woman in a tabard delivers a Zimmer frame.

Six-legged now, he bruises the paintwork as he moves. Stands at ease to block her escape from the bedroom or trap her in the kitchen.

Watching her, his tongue is wet against his bottom lip.

She waits for his mutation to full spider. Imagines them breaking in one day and finding her tightly wrapped in silk, teacup still raised to her mouth.

Simon Cowdroy

A Horse on the Roof and Other Stories

Our animals were all gone. Dad, and that 'damn cough' he couldn't shake, decided to rattle up a ladder and spend hours on the roof.

Robert, all of eighteen hands with a gentle heart, sweet face, and fifteen years dragging our plough weighing on every step, was last to go.

He whinnied as they struggled to load him, the stench of terror riding high in his nostrils. Dad whispered in his ear 'bout a better place, I stroked his muzzle one final time, Nana said, "s'pose you can't scrub the memory of fear out of knackery trucks."

Our house has the same smell most mornings.

I was down the back paddock this arvo, kicking up red dust in places where beautiful things used to grow, when a car pulled up.

They were frocked up like there was a funeral to get to. The woman checked my eyes, ears, and throat, before she wrapped a tape measure around one forearm.

The man was younger, kinder.

"Are you hungry?" he asked.

Dad said the words Ma told me never to use again and they hightailed it to their car like they'd trod on a bull ant nest.

They'll be back.

We sat on the hill behind our house as the sun gave up for another day.

"Wait for it," Dad said. "this'll be magic."

A brilliant moon rose above us, and the outline of a horse painted on the roof sparkled so brightly now that, hell, I was sure you could see it from Mars. Honestly, it looked more like a unicorn, but Dad had added a big 'R', so I'd know.

"Anytime now," he said. "Ma will fall from the stars and ride him back to heaven."

If I wish real hard maybe I could go too?

Nancy Ludmerer

Ski In/Ski Out

Because she vowed never to become a mother who said "because I say so" and because 15-year-old Nick argued constantly, and because that day in 1999 in Philadelphia it was about a ski trip to Whistler, British Columbia, and how he would never forgive her if she didn't say yes, and because his friends' parents all agreed their boys could go during the February break with two 19-year-old chaperones, and because she feared moguls and icy roads and the boys' collective judgment (or non-judgment), and because she foolishly mentioned avalanches, and because he smirked, "why not landslides, ma?" and stomped out, and because she wondered if she was unreasonable given he'd stopped smoking and was getting A's, which had earned him a direct phone line, including his own beige plastic wall phone, and because it started ringing and he wasn't there, and because, as her ex- said, she and Nick sounded interchangeable on the phone, she said "hello!" and a voice said, "Nicky! It's Brad. I'm in town, Holiday Inn on Walnut. Can we get together again?" and because this wasn't a 15-year-old voice or a 19-year-old voice but a 35 or 40-year-old voice, she managed, "This is Nick's mother. Who's this?" and because the voice continued pleasantly, "A colleague of his dad's. We met at his dad's place in New Hope," and because her voice unfroze then and she shouted, "Don't ever call him again, ever," and because after that, her heart pounding, she had still promised herself she would never be one to say "because I said so" and because she was certainly not going to be one who said "I told you so," she never told him, or anyone, about the phone call, and because of unrelated reasons, the trip to Whistler didn't happen.

Hannah Storm

A Linguistic Theory of Bats

We are in the college bar, drinking snakebite and black, you watching another match on TV, jumping and jeering like it's a matter of life or death. I'm trying to tell you my theory about the word for *bat* in different European languages and you think I'm talking about something to do with the game that has gone on all day, and I say not cricket bat: I'm talking about the flying kind and I reckon the words we use for these animals says something about our cultures. So, for instance, the French word is *chauve-souris* which translates as bald mouse, but before I can explain what this says about Gallic sensibilities, you say it's my turn to buy a round and anyway you can't concentrate with me rabbiting on. So, I leave you with the Italian *pipistrelle*, which is more romantic than its root word *vesper*, as in *night*, not Vespa as in I wish I could ride off into the sunset with someone who listens and loves me. And I head for the bar, thinking of the German *fledermaus*, or *flying mouse*, and how I should just take a leaf from this literal language and tell you we are *kaput*, when someone brushes my arm and says something which sounds like you could do better. He speaks so softly I have to lean in to listen, and I figure he looks and sounds Latino so I ask him if he knows what bat is in Spanish and flap my arms just in case. He smiles, all teeth and I imagine him sucking my blood, bringing me back to life. He mouths *mur-c-i-e-l-a-go*. It's the only Spanish word with every vowel, I say. And I know the fact it means *blind mouse* doesn't matter, because I can finally see.

Mark Ralph-Bowman

Dancing still

A whirring. He starts to move, rolling far away.

I feel a blurring of vision.

"Here."

There was his hand on my shoulder. I still feel it.

"Sit."

A tissue pulled from cellophane. Folded into a point, sharp as a needle. Eyeball to eyeball.

"Wide," he said. "Wider."

I spread the lids, tense, gaping, helpless, must have seemed in ecstasy.

All those years ago.

My mind now back at that beginning. Our life.

"Be still," he'd commanded.

"I'm trying," I'd whispered.

"There."

He held the point of the tissue before me, a microscopic black speck at its tip.

"It's gone," he said. "Nothing there now. You're fine – the pain will soon fade."

Soon it will fade. The dots and scratches, bunched tissues that mopped blood, sweat and tears; our unsteady videos of high days and low days, of running up and down Spanish Steps, whistling and weeping, in and out of temples, discos and toilets, getting ill, drawing salaries, pensions and heartbreak.

The grit of mortality. The bustle of it.

Polished beech wood, perfect beveled panels, the lines clean and square, geometric precision.

"The Classic French Beechwood casket," the man with a solemn smile had said. "Very popular."

Starlight flashes from the icy curlicues of brass.

Nimrod plays through the P/A.

I shift in my seat.

Then I see it. There. On the pearl-white petal of an Ice Caves lily – a tiny speck. A seed? An insect egg? A tiny grain? Minute.

Beyond, deep as space, a black hole swallows the remains of our time together as he plunges through the drapes. They swish behind this final act.

We hover about the floral displays and tributes, waiting to move on. From the chimney high above, smoke spirals, dancing.

Charlie Jones

Togashi-san

The final timber tumbled heavily into the fire beneath, sending a cloud of dancing sparks into the dark night. I watched them float up and away from the house, jolting and spurting on the heat from below. Papa held me tightly; my legs wrapped around his middle and my arms around his neck, neither of us able to look away. He had scooped me from my bed without waking me and hurried me out through the smoke-filled hall. We would be OK, he had panted. I would be safe, he had pleaded. But the fire trucks could do nothing to stop the flames destroying the dry wood of the old place, and as their red lights swung round and round, bouncing off the hats and boots of the firemen and the mirrored-wet ground, the house glowed brighter each minute until the white heat seared into my cheeks.

The last of my mother had been destroyed, there was no doubt of that; the pictures and letters now turned to smoke and filled my head and my nostrils. Papa was alone in remembering her alive. The smoke clung to him, his hair, his clothes. Desperate not to leave. I buried my head into his neck as deeply as I could and stayed there rocking slowly as he swayed from side to side, hushing me with whispers. I listened to the sirens and hummed along.

A lady gave me rice crackers and pulled a blanket around us. I watched the water run off the house and shimmer away down the hill. Papa began to sob. He had never held me like this before. I had never been so happy.

Ríbh Brownlee

[The Piano Burning]

I was with your friend when she set fire to her piano on that beach in England. At parties, she likes to tell the story as if she was alone. Sometimes, when she's meeting new people for coffee, she tells it as if her family was with her, helping her push the piano down the hill and rolling it across the road to get to the sand. In her story, her dad made jokes – *why did the piano cross the road?* – and waved at the cars that honked at them as they passed, all four of them pushing the piano like a pram.

She forgets that I was there. I remember helping her manoeuvre the piano through her living room doorway, laughing as it bashed into tables and bookshelves. It was an old upright and those keys that weren't missing were a stained yellow, like the colour of the walls in her childhood bedroom.

The way she likes to tell it – the burning of the piano – is that she started it by setting a length of driftwood on fire and holding it underneath the key bed until smoke rose and flowed out of the top board. She says that although the wood had a lavender burn, the piano flamed with an angry red. When she's drunk, she says that it was like nothing she had ever seen before; that smoke; that anger. It was incredible, otherworldly, almost mystical. She says that she stood and watched it until the sun went down away in the east.

It's a lovely story, but I was there. I saw her hands shake and wrapped my cardigan around her as she shivered. Then she left, leaving the great husk of a thing to burn by itself.

Linda Grierson-Irish

Crab Skeletons

Irfan knew a thing or two. Like how to pin a moth so it seemed forever in flight. That oxygen explodes out of stars. The rollercoaster journey a peanut makes from the oesophagus to the body's estuary. He knew these things from his best friend Joel's dad, who taught biology to the older kids at secondary.

Irfan knew other things too; things Joel's dad hadn't told him. That a man carrying a weight of whisky can fall further from a person's caring than a pebble flung from a cliff. That other fathers come home nights with mysteries up their sleeves, and wake their sons without anger when daylight hatches. Like Joel's dad. Who once almost died fighting the pull of the tide. Whose laughter was unpredictable like the sea.

"How'd you two boys like to come and collect crab skeletons tomorrow?" Joel's dad said.

"Don't go pestering Mr Franklin for too long," Irfan's mum told him, the Mothers-Pride-wrapped sandwiches and apples she packed saying different.

"So, Irfan, you're the man of the house now. 'Til your dad's well again." Irfan watched Joel's Dad's hands. Hands strong enough to haul the half-drowned lump of his father up the steep coastal path towards an on-the-way ambulance. He wanted to ask him was it okay to wish somebody dead. But then Joel's dad mightn't talk to him man to man anymore. Irfan pocketed his question for the stars. Some things he didn't need to know.

Joel's dad passed Irfan the specimen box to carry. Explained it was for the bones the crabs no longer needed. Irfan knew it didn't mean the crabs were dead. He imagined his father in the hospital, growing a fresh skeleton too. Side-stepping away from the old one for good. Becoming someone you might miss, without having to die.

Danny Beusch

One Day It Will All Bubble Over

Tuesday is curry night; sauce, from a tin, sieved to remove the sultanas.

"You want chips?" asks Dad.

"Of course," you reply. Stomach lining for later.

"That's my boy."

Dad dunks the potatoes into the pan, oil sizzling and hissing an inch beneath the rim. You flinch, every time.

"Don't be a girl," he says. "It's just water in the spuds."

You flash ID, thumb over the photo, and follow Ross across the crowded dancefloor to the room where darkness cloaks. Breathless grunting-cursing-moaning punctuates the bodies slapping, slippery as butter, and the relentless thumping bass. You feel the way: smooth face; chest slick with sweat; coarse hair below the navel; a button-up fly.

"You were late last night," Dad says. "Where'd you go?"

"Just a club."

"Isn't Tuesday night for poofs? You weren't with that Ross, were you?"

He turns his back to you, lowers the chip basket into the pan. A roar, like thunder. He lifts it out, stands an arm's length away, contorts his body from the spitting, angry fat. But today is different: too much water, or too much starch, or too much heat. The oil rises, thick and frothy, gushing over the top, down the sides, and onto the naked flame.

The look on his face: you never forget it. You tell your mates. You tell your fuck buddies. You tell your husband before he is your husband and his Guardian-reading folks. You tell your therapist and then, later, your social worker. And, in twenty years' time, you tell your son, who wriggles, giggles then leaps from your lap, pleading – please, please, pretty please – for silly old Grandad to make homemade chips for tea.

Krishan Coupland

A Grand Romantic Gesture

He is a skywriter. She doesn't love him. He's determined to win her back. The newspapers lap it up. Crowds point, take pictures, coo with delight. His little plane hums gamely over the city every afternoon for a week, spelling out messages in trails of smoke. SORRY and NOTHER CHANCE? and MISS YOU BAD. Each letter is the height of a football field.

She's gotten into the habit of not looking up. Not reading the papers. Her colleagues, however, are relentless. They congratulate her on each and every message.

"Don't you think it's romantic?" says one, perching on the edge of her desk and looking wistfully out at the blazing blue sky. "I'd give anything to have someone love me like that."

She sighs. "Even if you didn't love them back?"

The next day he writes FORGIVE ME. The day after I'M SORRY. There are pictures all over the internet. The weather shifts. His words become wobbly and brief. PLEASE he writes. CALL ME he writes. And then, one day, just her name, which dissolves almost instantly in a healthy breeze.

Her mother calls. "You simply must give him another chance. You're being obstinate. Almost cruel. Not just any man would do this for you." She hangs up without waiting for more. Feels her*self* dissolving. From the cupboard she fetches a tin of leftover paint. Out onto the fire escape she goes. Out and up, all the way to the roof. The day is blue and clear, almost perfect. The sun gleams off the roof. She pops the lid off the paint and sets to work writing, finally, a message of her own.

Nina Valentine

Roommates

His rusty red Chevy pulled into the drive as I took down the last stiff towel from the line. From his shaggy hair to the tattered t-shirt he tucked into belted work pants, I knew he was here for mom.

He certainly wasn't an insurance person here to look at my window, the dryer, or the leaky roof. Which was a shame. Winters here were brutal enough without a heater, but insurance was a luxury we couldn't afford.

I went inside and let the door slam shut behind me.

"Mom! For you!"

I didn't *have* to shout it. The trailer's walls were painfully thin. When she started bringing boyfriends over, I'd traded my monthly lunch allowance for a cheap pair of headphones from the corner store. That month was rough but it was well worth it.

Mom came out in a yellow sundress I'd never seen before. Her sandy blonde hair curled to frame her thin face and red lips. I ignored her, letting the basket of clothes drop onto the dark brown couch cushion for sorting.

A light rap on the door caught both of us by surprise. She opened it, smiling brilliantly at him.

"Hey! I'm ready." She grinned.

"Hey gorgeous! You didn't tell me you had a daughter. She gonna be okay alone?"

The question must have shocked her. Our eyes met. Hers seemed uncertain, worried, and sad. Silence filled the emptiness. I wanted to be angry and I couldn't.

"Andrea was just letting me crash here for a bit," I answered honestly. "I won't be around long, I promise."

They both smiled at that.

"That's Andrea for ya'! Heart like a saint."

"Yep, that's Andrea for you," I breathed.

He hugged her to him, pulling her out the door. It shut softly behind them, and latched.

Diane Simmons

Dancing

Robbie McMaster corners me after double maths.

"You ken we did the Gay Gordons in class the other day?" he says.

"Aye, you were great."

He does a wee bow. "I've been learning Scottish Country Dancing at the church hall every Thursday. We do Highland Dancing too. Do you want to come along?"

I hesitate and he goes awfie red.

"No' like that," he says. "I mean I'm no' asking you out or anything…"

I smile, tell him I ken whit he meant, but I dinnae answer his question. I'm fed up making excuses for no' doing things. And this is dancing. I bloody love dancing. "How much is it?"

"Only 75p."

I cannae imagine thinking 75p is nothing. I get £3 for doing my paper round and I've to pay everything out o' that. Maybe if I took on a Sunday round too? "Whit do the girls wear?" I ask.

"Your gutties and a skirt would do."

I picture myself turning up in ma plimsolls and school skirt, imagine the looks. "I dinnae think I can."

When I get to school the next day, there's a carrier on top of ma locker. Expecting something gross, I hold it away frae ma nose and peer inside – it's a pair of black dancing pumps.

I hound Robbie down at break. "I cannae take these," I say. "They must've cost a bomb."

"They were ma sister's," he says. "They dinnae fit anymore."

I examine the pumps again. There's no sign of any wear – there's no' a single mark on them. He must think I'm daft.

"That's awfie nice of your sister," I say. I stare at the pumps, then at Robbie's worried face and grin at him. "See you there on Thursday," I say.

"Seven o'clock," he says, and grins back.

Alison Woodhouse

Bad Blood

Here I am, dated and pasted between thin plastic sheets, pressed and smoothed in the red leather album from Grandma's house.

I'm the girl with the pudding bowl hair, gap-toothed, arms splayed, up against the wall where the pear tree droops. My sandals are sticky with sweet rotting fruit and the wasps are biting.

I'm the girl with hyacinth eyelids, wobbly strawberry lines around my mouth, dusty pink kisses on my cheeks. Downstairs, she whacks her ruler across the back of my hands, twice. *My room is out of bounds,* she says, *and nice girls don't wear make up.*

I'm the girl on the back seat of the Zephyr 4 parked outside her front door, my Sunday dress too tight across my chest. Grandma's cigarette is clamped tight between her lips and she's looking elsewhere.

Where's the photograph of the raggedy lobed hawthorn and purple sloes flying past the car window and the hundredth time of my mother saying *she was a kind woman, wasn't she?*

Where's the picture of Grandma's house never smelling of bread and blackberry jam, just empty shells and a stiff north-easterly?

Or the shoreline where I walk, smoking in quick inhalations like a beached fish gulps air.

I hang back as our little family tramps up the gravel path to St. Botolphs, but there's no photograph of me sucking blood from my thumb, ravenous.

Are you alright, my mother asks, but maybe not then, maybe much, much later.

When they finish lowering Grandma into the freshly dug hole, I step to the precipice, turn out my pockets. Shell shards tumble and so do my cigarettes but no one sees, they're too busy slinging mud.

I don't cry, oh no, not until Mother's thin arms lasso me, and then I am gasping.

Emma Kentish

The Cards

Mother played patience, painted nails clicking, a sliding jingle of bracelets along her wrists. A cigarette lay burning. At her elbow, a glass and a bottle of brandy. I knew that any questions had to come before the label. After the neck but before the label.

Questions had to be timed to a win as well. With a satisfied nod she swept the cards into a crisp pile, the stack fluttering from one hand to the other.

"Where is my father?"

Mother arched an eyebrow, one eye crinkling against the smoke. She peered down her long nose at me as if surprised by my courage.

"Earl's Court," she answered. I could only wonder where this 'Earl's Court' might be. In whose palace, in what land?

Mother fanned through the cards and plucked out two black queens to lay on the table, then two red queens. She picked out the joker and placed it above the row of queens.

"Your father," she said, her voice gravelly, smoke streaming out of both nostrils.

"With his harem."

I looked at the cards, then up at my mother. Her head tilted to one side as if she too was puzzled. I was bursting with questions. What is a harem? What's a court? But I knew not to fidget, not to seem to be there at all.

"He knows about you."

She crushed the spent cigarette and poured a drink, below the label now. The next sip might turn her voice to a snarl, see her lunge across the table and flick my head with sharp fingernails.

Streetlights striped my bed. I lay tight, scared of multi-coloured queens and joker's bells. I thought instead about the friendly cracks in the ceiling snaking a route to the Earl's Court.

Sally Pearson

Cracker

"Try this," she says, passing it to him.

Once, he would have smiled, said 'thank you'. Now he clasps the flat, crisp circle with clawed hands. She's worried he won't have the strength to find the breaking point.

A push of thumbs, a twist of wrists — click! Relief as it snaps.

She sees his arm shake as he lifts one half of the cracker to his mouth. His lips close on the dimpled surface, gums edging together, coaxing it into saliva. A pause while the morsel goes soggy. She offers him a creamy slice of goat's cheese, pungent on wax paper; watches while he squashes it into his mouth, presses with his tongue, lets his palate do the work. She imagines his taste buds flooding with the rich, country flavour.

She's pleased he can still feed himself — despite the wasted muscles, wheelchair, the indignity of stinking nappies. She pushes the blue beaker with its baby spout closer. His fingers, trembling, curl around the handle. He lifts, tips, manages a single slug of blood-red liquid. She wipes a burgundy dribble from the corner his mouth, tracks it across the grizzled chin.

Her own life is one of spinning plates, all speed. A demanding boss, kids, dirty linen, a stressed, unemployed partner. But today she's left work early, finished the shopping, taken two buses to the cabbage-smelling care home to be with him.

A bell rings. Their time is up, but the silent telly in the corner is flashing news.

"That dreadful virus again. It's reached Italy now! Don't worry Dad, it won't get over here." She stands to leave, bends down to kiss him. "See you next week?"

Has he heard? He raises his head, tries to speak. Her heart jumps. For a second it seems he knows her.

Claire Boot

Teulu

"Oes teulu gyda chi?"

Do you have family? A simple enough question, Sandra scolded herself. Evening classes weren't meant to cause an existential crisis. She knew she'd have to make something up for the exam and pray she didn't get caught out.

"Oes teulu gyda chi?" repeated Richard, his new varifocals forcing him to circle his head over the textbook like some sodding nodding dog.

Sandra had tried. She'd asked the tutor, Rhiannon, the Welsh word for cousin, but it wouldn't stick in her head.

"Mae cyf – cef – mae cyfn –"

God, how she envied people who could answer easily.

"Mae dau o blant gyda fi," she heard Jo say brightly from the desk behind.

I have two children.

Funny that, thought Sandra, how plant means children. She had lots of potted plants lining the windowsills of her flat. She'd grown some from seed, one from a date stone, and sprouted enough aloe veras to suffocate a small yoga studio. Did plants count as family?

Richard pulled a handkerchief from his trouser pocket and took off his glasses. He scrubbed the lenses, realising too late that the handkerchief wasn't entirely clean.

Sandra focussed on the question in the textbook. She liked what it really asked in Welsh. Not do you *have* family, not do you own or possess, but is family *with* you?

Yes, of course – Mam, Tad, y babi bach – Mum, Dad, the little baby. She didn't have any of them anymore, not in the English sense. But, in the Welsh way, yes, they were always with her.

"Oes teulu gyda chi?" persisted Richard. He glanced imploringly at Rhiannon, but she was busy writing irregular verbs on the whiteboard with the wrong sort of marker pen.

"Oes," Sandra smiled decisively at Richard. "Mae teulu gyda fi."

L.J. Moss

Stone Girl

Curiosity. That was the start of it. In these long hours and days I spend here now, wrapped in a mantle of stone, I think about that. There is so much to regret, and yet, and yet…

Take the small decanter, three shelves down, thirty degrees to the left, add essence of sulphur, an egg plucked from the nest of a nightingale at dawn and seven drops of the purest mountain dew. Stir it clockwise for six turns by the light of a waxing moon…

On and on she'd go, giving me tasks that seemed never-ending, while she became whatever she wanted to be, an eagle, a trout, a horse, even a leopard, once. Off she'd fly, or gallop or swim, and a few days later she'd be back – exhilaration all over her face…

And I cleaned the workshop.

Peeled potatoes for stew.

Fed the pigs.

And brewed *her* another potion.

And then. I stuck my littlest finger in the potion and licked it clean. Started small: became Mouse. Next night, Rat. After that, Cat. Dog. Horse. And my favourite: Bird.

Each night I was bolder. I got a taste for the potion and took it more and more often. Who amongst mortals never wondered what it would be like to shapeshift into the body of another creature…

… my vision, needle sharp, leaving the earth behind, body light, light with the hollow bones of a hawk, weightless and soaring in a sky full of bright stars… Once you've tasted magic,

licked its unbearable sweetness from your lips, felt it fizz and
sparkle on your tongue, there's no going back.

Not to clean the workshop.

Peel potatoes for stew.

Feed the pigs.

And brew *her* another potion.

Wrapped in a mantle of stone, I think about that.

Nikki Crutchley

Contagious

"It's Jeremy's," I say, fingering the lapel of the jacket that hangs off my frame.

"Oh, how … nice."

It's not 'nice.' Her tone tells me so, the way her hand drops from my shoulder, as if not wanting to catch my special kind of grief.

"You should take it to the Salvation Army. They're in desperate need of good clothes."

I wonder when she would realise that this clenched lip smile, feigned interest relationship between us was only ever held together by him.

The trip has taken just under two hours. On the way I gave myself talking points, what to avoid (anything to do with Jeremy, or anything Jeremy liked, or cancer – hell, just death and dying in general), and what to talk about (gardening, cooking, The Living Channel).

Jeremy didn't realise what he was doing that day when, towards the end, he asked me to keep an eye on his mother.

"She has no one else."

But what about me? I had wanted to scream.

I stand outside The Salvation Army and watch as a decapitated mannequin is manhandled into the jacket, a 'V' of beige, muscular chest on show as buttons are secured. He fills it out better than me, but not as well as Jeremy.

I think of the person who buys it, unaware of the two lives it's already lived: worn by Jeremy a few times a week; on weekends at parties, spilt beer and cigarette smoke; minute pin pricks from a barrage of boutonnières over years of wedding seasons; a shelter for summer storms. And its second life with me, tucked into my breast each night, my grief in every stitch.

I walk back into the shop. My fingers hover on the smooth plastic chest and then I undress him.

Karen Jones

Unscrewed

The couple in the hotel room next to mine alternate between screaming at each other or playing bhangra music so loud, I half expect a Bollywood cast to seep through the walls. That would be a welcome diversion from my room service meal of macaroni cheese and bottle of red wine – yes, a whole bottle, just for me, what of it? – their dazzling beauty and sparkling costumes a relief from the beige walls, beige towels and beige thoughts in this room. Room 101. Oh, how I didn't laugh at that one, but he would have – he who didn't meet me here, who made the reservation, who promised one of his promises and who doesn't actually like hotels or beige or, as it turns out, me. I wonder if he likes bhangra, likes sequins, likes that unscrewing-the-lightbulb move I find so charming in Bollywood dances? He likes screaming – I remember that much – but would he like this screaming, in a language we don't understand, with a soundtrack too jaunty for the pain in the argument hammering through the wall?

There's crying now. The music softens. Voices plead and plait together in sorrow and love. Funny how you can hear love even if you don't know the words wailed through sobs over dhol and zither.

I check my phone one last time for reasons, excuses and future promises, see cheese stains on my blouse – sloppy eater, sloppy mother, sloppy wife, sloppy lover. Red wine tinged lips smile at me in the mirror. The music cranks up a notch to cover the sound of reconciliation. I stand, bend my knees, toes pointed outwards, arms raised, elbows bent, chin tilted upwards, ready to bounce on my heels, reaching for imaginary blown out bulbs to unscrew. I close my eyes and dance.

Patricia Q. Bidar

Kitties

Shirley's mother struck a motherlode of pastel capris at the swap meet. But the pants are too small. Loud Aunt Lola, staying until her divorce is through, wants to try them. In the guest bedroom, Aunt Lola drops her jean shorts. Shirley rushes to close the door. On either side of Aunt Lola's underpants, the black bush explodes. Shirley has seen her mother's down-below hair in the bathtub with Baby Teo. Mama's kitties, Shirley and her sister called it. But that was years ago.

Aunt Lola only sees her three children every other weekend. On the bed sits a collection of candy—three of everything.

Two women. Six children. Two kitties. One marriage, ripped wide like a bag of sweets.

Shirley's developing early. On the phone with her girlfriend, her mother refers to Shirley as "awfully mature." The two Carries at school have taken her aside to tell her that she needs a bra. For now, she wears her bathing suit top under her Hang Ten t-shirt.

After a few cans of Coors, Aunt Lola always says that Uncle Bill smacked her around. No one believes her, including Shirley's parents.

Alone in the bathroom while the family sleeps, Shirley smears Nair on her kitty. The smell is awful. It burns and the sulphur stink clings. But for a few days, Shirley's kitty is smooth like before.

Then the area begins to itch. The hair grows back, itching and prickly. Before long, Shirley's kitties are back. She checks the bathroom, but her mother's Nair is gone. She will need to steal a tube from Thrifty Jr. after school. Then, to be certain, she will sleep with the Nair on her kitties. She will not move, no matter how much it burns. She will not move until they are gone for good.

Carmen Price

Fake Ferns

Hilda was a goldfish who knew her days were numbered, but she wasn't afraid of death. She'd listened to the woman beyond the glass tell her friends that they couldn't actually live if they kept searching for the meaning of life, or kept worrying about dying, and that had been enough for Hilda's peace of mind. But the same couldn't be said of Hyacinth – the Cherry Barb with whom Hilda shared a tank. Hyacinth had listened to the woman beyond the glass, too, but on a different day, when the woman beyond the glass had read aloud to her friends from a big book that had made them all laugh. Ever since, Hyacinth had raced back and forth through the cloudy water, completely ignoring Hilda, muttering about fish seeking death and not finding it, about fish-children being killed with death, about beasts full of eyes within.

"She's not serious," Hilda had pleaded with Hyacinth, bacterial bloom sifting in and out of her gills, "she's just joking…they're all joking."

But had they been joking?

One morning, when Hilda expected to find food, she found Hyacinth floating in the film at the top of the tank. Hyacinth's death wasn't a surprise – Cherry Barbs didn't live very long, everybody knew that – and Hilda didn't suspect anything other than natural causes. But when a colossal hand scooped Hyacinth from the water like a child plucking up the last bit of candy from the bottom of a bag, Hilda was overcome with a sense of dread as cold and empty as Hyacinth's lifeless eyes.

Hilda swam to the other side of the tank.
She hid behind the fake ferns.

Amelia Butterly

The Dentist's Drill

"This weekend," my dentist said to the nurse, "I'm putting up shelves in the living room." The nurse had spring cleaning to do, she replied, dusting and vacuuming. I, with a mouth full of metal instruments, said nothing.

"Next time you'll need a filling," the dentist told me as I left.

A few weeks later, I found myself back in his chair. He showed me the drill before he put it in mouth. Out in the room, it had seemed small and harmless, buzzing humorously. Inside my mouth, it felt like a squad of workers had taken up residence, carrying out the kind of serious repairs that caused water mains to be switched off and traffic to tail back miles. The nurse pushed the suction against my gum and asked the dentist about his new DIY plans. Kitchen cabinets, he replied.

I returned a month before my next check-up, with a throbbing that had kept me awake most of the night. I screwed up my eyes in pain, while he examined my mouth, tapping teeth with a hammer. The nurse left the room briefly, to sign for a package.

"That'll be my carpentry materials," the dentist said to me. "I'm afraid there's a lot of work."

I returned the next day for a two-hour appointment. He began his latest project. The drills and hammers were joined by sanders, screwdrivers and what I feared could only be pliers. The radio blared out 80s tunes and the dentist hummed along as he worked. "Not much longer now," he said, a little sadly. The minutes ticked by slowly.

Eventually he put the chair upright. I rinsed. "Open wide," he said. "Let me admire my work."

I gaped, lips splitting at the sides.

"Now, I'd like to see you again next week."

Jill Varani

Mount Kailash

The Bottle-O man nodded at Tara as she entered. His eyes glinted. Recognition, or just a reflection of all that glass? She thought he didn't know her name yet. She knew he had a family he didn't see and a dream of moving to Tibet. He was bald with a long grey beard and teeth that seemed to grow in all directions. When he smiled she always thought he might cry.

She picked two bottles of wine and brought them back to the counter. "How are you?" she said, hiding her hands so he wouldn't see them tremble.

"Bored," he said.

"Is it boring here?"

"You see the same people all the time. Even by the cars that pull up outside, I know who's coming in. Always the same people."

"How long have you worked here?"

"Six years. It's a family business you know."

"I didn't know."

"I will sell it. In two years."

"And move to your mountain."

"You know, Miss Tara." He smiled his tears. "Mount Kailash." He pointed to the photo of the mountain that he kept sellotaped to the edge of his screen. The mountain was almost round and bare of trees, iced with snow. Like a cake.

She didn't have a family either, but she never told him that. Perhaps he guessed. When the fires came, she didn't have anybody else to wonder about. Was he insured? Did he get to his mountain? She tried to find out – newspapers, Google. She phoned the police. They couldn't tell her much. There were still a lot of missing people.

She thought he must have made it. She imagined him climbing up. His frosted beard. That smile. His breath like smoke before him.

He had told her once that from Mount Kailash you could hang the world.

Dawn Gallery

No-one will be able to hear me

We make our own entertainment between teatime and bedtime. Mum doesn't like us getting under her feet while she's trying to get the dishes done before Coronation Street starts. And Dad likes his tea and fig rolls in peace. They've both had a hard day at work, and we're a handful.

There are seven of us running as fast as we can through the long grass in the playing fields. I try ever so hard to keep up with the others but I've only got little legs. Dad says he's seen better hanging out of a sparrow's nest. And I have to do my little dance every few steps, or otherwise the daddy long legs will get up my trousers, and I don't like that. I look like someone is shooting at my feet, like they do in the Cowboy Films. The others threaten to leave me behind if I don't hurry up. So I'd better get a move on.

Usually I am only allowed to be an Indian because I haven't got a gun. Dad says I might get one for my birthday though if I'm a good girl for a change. But tonight Michael says that I can be a cowboy if I do as I'm told. I've got to stand still and stop squirming while they tie me to the lamppost, as there are no trees on our estate like there were in olden times America. He says they have captured me, and they will scalp me, and I will be a baldy. And then they will set a fire and dance around me. Michael says no one will be able to hear me screaming and crying over the sound of their TVs, so I might as well shut my face.

Marie Gethins

Echoes

My mother's bed has an alarm. On the door, a sign says: FALL RISK. I'm in a pale blue vinyl chair giving the same responses; the billionth time we're having this looped conversation. I should wear a tag that says: FLIGHT RISK.

The doctor makes his rounds. "You're the daughter that lives in Ireland?" Bedside Manner 101. He gives stats and estimates, then takes my place in the dialogue circle. Checks complete, he smiles and edges out backwards. Her lost cynicism in my head: "Fine for some."

I watch worried fingers rearrange objects on her bed tray. A miniature tissue box slides from one corner across to another, the fuchsia sippy cup takes its place.

"Why am I here?"

"When can I go home?"

"Why am I here?"

My reading a paperback annoys her, but phone scrolling does not. I text friends back home, exchange slivers of dark humour. More Irish than the Irish, although my accent gives me away.

A nurse with a multitude of thin braids comes to take blood. My mother admires the hairstyle. How long did it take? Did she do it herself? As I listen, shoulders ease into blue vinyl. "Honey, you sure have been poked and prodded," the nurse says. Her rubber clogs beat a soft exit.

"Why am I here?"

"When can I go home?"

I auto reply, one ear attuned to the hall. Food trolleys. Case murmurs. Alarm pulses. "Right, fair enough." The accent pulls me out of the chair and to the door. A nurse leans on the counter, phone pressed to her ear. I want to shout, "Cork!" To talk of tidal barriers and recent snow, of Shandon bells and the English Market. To revel in my chosen present with a stranger and abandon the past where I currently stand.

Dionne McWilliams

The First Wave

Nasim pauses on the steps of the masjid to inhale the warm, full air of the early evening. Smoke infused with charred lamb and cumin stings his eyes gently as he searches for his shoes.

Yaman catches his eye and wades towards him through the sea of crouching men. They embrace, and their hands naturally find each other in a gesture of friendship and brotherhood. They walk, clasped hands swinging loosely between them, weaving expertly through the crowded square.

"How is Salima?"

Nasim unconsciously squeezes his friend's hand in response. He is dying to tell Yaman his news, but he has promised his wife that their pomegranate seed-sized blessing will remain their secret for at least another three weeks. "She's fine." Yaman glances expectantly at his friend, and sees that he should change the subject. "Will you come to Reza's match on Thursday?" he asks. "It's his first game for the under-16s".

The friends stroll on, conversation jumping from the amazing goalkeeping skills of Yaman's brother, to Nasim's upcoming accountancy exams, to today's local news. The town was buzzing again with rumours that Abu Bakr al-Hamani was seen arriving late the previous night. Nothing unusual; the coordinator of the US Embassy attack in the capital was the subject of more sightings than Elvis.

A bat makes an uncomfortably low swoop overhead as they pass the fruit stall, piled high with over-ripe apricots. Both cower, and they mock their mutual overreaction.

They stop to pet the stray cat that has been resident in the doorway of the derelict hotel for the last week. Nasim would love to take it home, but Salima is afraid of bringing parasites into their spotless lives. Especially now.

Directly above them, a swarm of silent drones releases the first wave of missiles onto the target.

Hema Nataraju

Curse of the Marble Carver

They cut our thumbs off after our work is done.

The Padshah ensures there will never be another Taj Mahal.

After years of carving the sun and moon on buttery marble, my hands know nothing else. Now I draw on parchment, over and over, quill between my index and middle fingers. The sun for the Emperor, moon for the state.

On marble, the moon couldn't be anywhere close to the sun, but on parchment, Moon refuses to be a thin fingernail. I let it take over. It puffs up, claiming its space. It swallows Sun whole.

I hear that the Padshah's son has imprisoned him. Victorious Moon laughs with me.

Christina Eagles

Pierrot

Pedro cleans his nails with a sheath knife as he sits in the Big Top waiting for the clowns to arrive for rehearsal. Once he was proud of his clean hands, his neat and polished nails. Fog drops off these northern hills and he shivers inside his pierrot costume. Last night's show limped, the timing slipshod. The others do not care about this as he does.

He allows himself to watch Jarek stroll into the tent, climb to the trapeze in the canvas roof. This might be the last time he sees how Jarek's calves flex as his feet thrust against each rung.

Was it Katja who tended that glistening skin this morning? When he and Jarek shared the yellow caravan it was Pedro's task to smooth oil across that back, around the slopes of thigh and bicep. Pedro's fingers remember each dip and hollow, the places where the muscles knot.

His knife slips, skids towards his palm. He curses as he sucks at a line of blood droplets scored along his finger.

Pedro has considered telling Katja about Jarek's wife and son in Poland. They may, he knows, be no more real than the illusion of flying when Jarek swoops from one trapeze to the other. Jarek's words drop like rain into the sea, lost even as they fall. Only those gleaming shoulders, the contours of the sculpted calves, are solid.

The clowns waver across the sawdust at last and Pedro's knife drops as he stands to meet them, its tip spearing the ground. The quivering blade conjures up another image. As he cajoles the team through their tired routines he cannot keep his mind from prodding at the picture, the frayed ends of a half-sawn rope.

Above him, Jarek's trapeze groans as it swings.

Alpheus Williams

Harmless Lies

The legless man on the skateboard scoots across the street, positions himself against the wall of a curio shop and places a small bucket for donations. He posts no sign. It's illegal. Those who can see him don't need a sign to get the message, for those who need a sign he's invisible anyway.

Dark stubbled cheeks, hair lank and oily. He might be middle aged. It's hard to tell. Life on a skateboard is tough.

The legless man tells those who express an interests that he lost his legs in the war. When they ask which war, he's evasive. He tells them it's too painful to talk about.

It's a harmless lie. He was born without legs. His life has been a constant war but he didn't have to kill anyone or leave home to fight it.

Welcome. Thank you. God bless, he says as coins tinkle into the bucket. He doesn't believe in God. It's another harmless lie but it hurts no one and that's the truth of it.

Antoinette Bauer

Hungary, 1956

I want to try on for size my father's body, inhabit, his seven-year old boy body. And so, I do. I slip on his boy skin, his boy muscles, boy everything.

Immediately, I feel lithe and free.

I am climbing, climbing, high walls and high branches; jumping and landing the pommel horse, the bar, everything in the gymnasium, my second home. At school, I shine brassy gold with brilliant potential. A wunderkind of stretching, connecting synapses that are going to take me away, away from my scratch on the map village.

My new limbs know no limits and neither do I, yet. I am free as a boy happy in his own buoyed skin and scuffed shins.

I run to my house and my mama. She cooks for me, dumplings. To feed is to love me. I try not to choke on my own hunger for life. I am seven, you see.

By fourteen I am becoming my father's son. Muscles and hair sun-bronzed in the hard chair I sit tall with responsibilities.

My little sister is a lovely pest. Night and day, under my feet. But when I'm gone, I'll miss her pesky ways.

In my unimagined future, I will ask my love to try on clothes to send to my sister in a package.

At last, inhabiting my father's young man skin, I arrive. A student in big smoke Budapest, my eyes fill up with the classic beauty surrounding me and the fireworks of exploding new everything. At home, a family waits for their golden-haired son to one day return filled with light, lithe, ascending weightless.

I never saw you again my one and only sister, but did you see it? Did my package filled with missing you, missing home, ever arrive?

Michael Mcloughlin

Birthday Present

Alicia can sense a storm is on the way. If rain stops work she won't be able to pick her daily quota of 100 kilos at 50c per kilo. She'd pick in the rain if she could, in a storm, but the boss won't allow that: picking in the rain causes bruising to the fruit. Bruising strawberries is a no-no, three strikes and you're out.

Her friend, Maria, calls out, "You see Batchelor last night?"

"Yeah, maybe he prefers fruit picker like us."

Maria laughs… "You think it will rain?"

"Hope not, want to buy Rafael birthday present."

Alicia stands up to stretch her aching back. She checks the sky and can sense the storm is getting closer. But something isn't right: three white vans fast approaching. Almost in unison, the other pickers stop and look over. The banter falls to silence. They watch in their crouched positions as the vans get closer, eyes fixed. Then they all stand as the vans speed towards them and screech to a halt. The doors bust open. Maria shouts, "*Inmigración!*" She takes off across the field with the other pickers, strawberries flying like splattered blood – but Alicia doesn't move. Confused. Grabbed. She's hauled away, along with the remaining pickers.

Just as she's handled into the van by a Homeland Security officer, she stops and looks straight into the camera, guessing she'll be on the news. She will be, but it won't be to tell the viewers that it's her son's third birthday today.

Nicola Ashbrook

The Gravitational Pull of Cooper Jeffries

I drive two extra miles to re-fuel my car because of him. He mans the till – not a doctor as I used to imagine – but still Elvis-handsome. Always a hint of pinprick stubble; top button wantonly splayed. The name etched on my heart also etched on a badge skimming his left nipple.

He still doesn't say much, apart from "£45 please," and "Nectar card?" but his eyes… I think about what those heavily-lashed babies say whenever I'm alone. Whenever.

The Saturday after our honeymoon we're out-out with friends. I've had a couple of Jager bombs; my legs are nicely woolly. Daniel kisses me as he lumbers back to the bar and I'm thinking how bloody loved-up we are when in He comes.

"Hey," he says.

I'm sixteen immediately. He's just snogged Melissa Brent behind the science block and I'm My So Called Life level devastated.

Muted, I just nod.

I'm in third lesson Maths, a year before the Melissa Brent incident, when He glides over. I almost hyperventilate when he folds into the chair beside me.

"Alright?" he asks, from beneath a better side-fringe than mine.

He doesn't say much and he's copying my answers but his elbow occasionally knocks mine; his knee rests thrillingly against my thigh.

The other girls all have cropped tops but my mum insisted I need a bra. He's the first to notice, to laugh loudly, alerting the class as he twangs the strap against my back.

I blush, but mostly because he touched me.

We meet at the electric pencil sharpener on the first day of school.

"I'll do it for you," he says, making my Care Bear pencil the sharpest it's ever been.

"Thanks Cooper, I'll love you forever now!" I gush.

And I will. I really will.

Karen Ashe

No thanks, I just ate lunch

It was 4pm. Bernadette arrived just as the maid was serving up dessert, a three-tier affair dripping with chocolate mirror-glaze. May have been shop-bought. Hard to tell.

"No thanks," she said, lowering herself into the chair beside mine. "I just ate lunch."

"Still wearing the Spanx, huh?"

"Yup. Three more days and I can take 'em off."

A newly-arrived from England remarked that they had had no idea that you could get liposuction in the Philippines, and Bernadette said, "Oh sure, and so much cheaper than here in Hong Kong. And just as good." She's been very open about her decision to have the procedure. Her mother was a Playboy Bunny, so she's no stranger to bit of remodelling, haha. "But I really am done now. I'm done, I'm done, I'm definitely done."

Next time I saw her was lunch in a restaurant. "Idiot that I am, I got my dates mixed up, and thought this was next week! So I already ate lunch! I will have dessert though! They have this darling little chocolate caramel something, and I'll have a coffee as well," she told the quite-confused waitress "but decaf; can you imagine me on caffeine? Haha!"

When I came back from the bathroom, she was telling everyone about a procedure a woman at the gym had had done. "They make a slit under your eye and suck out all the crud that gives you bags and dark circles. But I'll be done after that. One more and I'm done. And it's a great excuse for a trip to the Philippines, am I right ladies?"

When the waitress arrived with the dessert and decaf, she remembered she needed to make a quick call and she went outside so as not to disturb everyone and by the time she was done the coffee was cold and the dessert was a congealed mass. But it was fine, because she was full anyway. She'd just had lunch.

Vera Sofia

Nowhere near

While Aya is crossing the Mediterranean, Zoe wakes up in Berlin. She looks at the Bode Museum through the window with a cup of coffee in her hands searching for reasons to face the day. She is tired, too tired.

While Zoe parks her car swearing about the traffic, Aya prays for the boat to land.

Zoe arrives at her workplace cursing the day she accepted her CEO promotion. She doubts all the choices she made in life, she doubts of life itself.

Aya has nothing but life. So she doesn't doubt. She believes in Europe: she will find a way to Berlin, the city she once heard as 'the future'; she will have a job, a flat, a car; she will be safe.

While Zoe is taking her pills to sleep wishing to never wake up again, Aya is sinking on the Mediterranean waters.

Zoe will wake up cross with life. Feeling tired, too tired. Aya will never cross Italy or France or Switzerland to get to Berlin. Zoe will never get to herself.

Anna Giangiordano

Portrait of a Younger Man

Harding hasn't thought of Seeley for three decades, nearly four, but something in the portrait of a man he bought at auction, with little more thought than that he liked it, was Seeley, perhaps smiling at him.

The portrait takes up the whole of the chimney breast, suns itself like a cat in the light from the window at the back of the house. The subject is wearing jeans, torso bare, ash hanging dangerously on the tip of the cigarette held between faintly yellowed fingers, and behind him a zebra stripe of blinds, a cheese-plant, and sunlight bright as butter.

Harding is intrigued and faintly repulsed that the painting ends at the man's white and freckled shoulders.

The painted man watches him, Harding is sure. That scrutiny makes him skittish and shy which is inconvenient and annoying at his age. He's a fool but he still stands at the foot of the painting, and sips hot coffee in the mornings, remembering how he sat at Seeley's feet, in their rooms at college and watched the sun slide like a scalpel across his lover's skin.

Mourning Seeley thirty-eight years ago had been a stoic, unsatisfactory event.

Harding kneels because he can no longer stand, and places his coffee mug precisely on the floor; the process of grief giving into the practical. This done, he puts his hands over his face and cries.

A fortnight will bloom into three weeks, into four, before he can present himself again, puffed up with embarrassment, muffled by the need to apologise.

A.J. Bolton

Killing Time

I can't sleep so I count the eerie whistling from the ventilator next door. Inhale. Exhale. I get to sixteen, when she erupts into deep vulgar coughing. Her assistance light comes on. I stop listening then.

Blue sheets stick to my damp thighs, comfort evades me. I watch the woman asleep in the far corner. She's drooling on herself. I wonder about her dreams, happy ones or nightmares?

There's a wide ugly breathing tube cut into her throat which she chokes on often through the night. The first three times I panicked and called for help, but they didn't seem too worried. I stopped worrying too.

They come in and pull the curtains around next door's cubicle. Her coughing has ceased. They say;

"*Time to change you, Lakshmi.*"

I sink into my own revolt. The room fills with the pungent, putrid smell of two-day old shit. My eyes water and I can taste it, I want to vomit. I pinch my nose and breath only through my mouth.

I don't belong here; I feel like a fraud. My mind tells me this, although my body says differently. I welcome the ticking of the clock marking the death of seconds, minutes, hours. But I simultaneously fear the same thing. White coats tell me things, words I'm not ready to understand. It's been twenty-three days now, and I'm going numb.

Better than everything hurting, I suppose.

The cubicle opposite me is empty now. The girl who occupied it was quiet and pale. A young one. They moved her so quickly in the middle of the night with all her monitors beeping.

I don't know what happened to her, I didn't ask.

I had learnt that was the best way.

Kathryn Aldridge-Morris

It's not what happens to you

My foster mum said I had eyes bigger than my belly, and I used them to look sideways into Jane Patterson's lunchbox. When I saw what I saw, my bobble elastic snapped and my bunches started spinning like a candyfloss machine. *Cucumber*. But not in slices. And not in sandwiches. Cut up in sticks. All the same size and in their *own* little lunch box. She saw me and smiled. Jane Patterson was voted friendliest girl at the end of last term. I ignored her and went straight to my Wagon Wheel.

"You having that before your crisps?"

"I always have pudding first."

Jane nodded and poured water from the metal jug into her pink metal beaker.

"Is it true you were one of the robots in the Smash makes Mash advert?"

"Uh huh. Got a million pounds for it," I spluttered, biscuit spraying her smooth hair.

"My dad says that's crap," Matthew Butler butted in.

"Your dad's a doctor. What does he know about show business?"

"At least I've –"

"Actually. My dad's a deep-sea diver for an oil rig off the coast of Wiltshire."

I put some crisps into my mouth, still chewing on the last mouthful of Wagon Wheel. Jane giggled and pushed her Penguin into her mouth, still full of cucumber.

"And is it true you drank two snow globes?" asked Jane.

"Three."

"What happens to the bits inside?"

"It's snow. They melt. Inside your pooh."

Jane walked home with me after school. When I got in, I watched real mum open a tin of corn beef hash.

"Jane Patterson gets cucumber rectangles."

Without speaking, she swung the tin-opener across my face. My eye went black as a jawbreaker. But going to Accident & Emergency was okay, really. I went by flying saucer.

Robert Scott

Breakfast Menu Guy – A Question

I see this guy every morning on the way from my crappy bedsit to my crap retail job.

He shouts out the menu for a cooked breakfast: sausages, fried eggs, mushrooms, bacon, tomatoes – the lot. Pretty loud. Louder than the rush hour traffic. I see him on my way home, too, doing the same thing. He doesn't seem to have a teatime menu.

The other thing he does is slap the walls as he walks along, which is like something a little kid would do.

They're shutting down the local 'mental hospital', as most people call it. And trying to empty out the patients before they knock the place down, or turn it into flats, or whatever. I suppose Breakfast Menu Guy's one of them.

I had a good pal in that place, but I wouldn't tell you anything about that, except that last I heard he was doing all right.

I danced with a nurse from there once, late on in a club. We were both pretty pissed. She appeared out of nowhere, like a siren from the mists – sort of. A few weeks later, I was getting a bus to my old village and I saw her sitting up front, her uniform collar showing under her coat. She got off at the hospital stop.

Back to my friend with the breakfast menu in his head. My question is this: what should I do? You know, I haven't got any money, but I've got some free time; when I'm not at my crappy job. No family responsibilities. What can I do for this guy? Say hello? Try a chat? He doesn't seem to see me when I walk past him. What should I do?

No one tells you that shit.

Kate O'Grady

Kilburn Wedding, 1962

Our squashed wedding cake was the third bad omen. My father, already tipsy, wiped Victoria sponge from the backside of his best trousers, and shouted "who the feck left it on the armchair?" My mother, sporting curlers as big as Swiss rolls, shrieked once and then calmly told my sister to "run around to Lyons and get another one quick."

"Sorry love", my father said, and poured another Jamison's.

"We'll sort it out love," my mother said, and the smile she gave me was as big and wide and hopeful as a sunflower. Then she ran water from the tap, soaked a tea towel and told my father, to bend over.

My dress and veil hung in the wardrobe. Two white clouds trapped inside a small, dark space. "Bride," I would say to myself each time I looked at them, the weight of the word heavy on my tongue.

I had fallen hard for your shamrock coloured eyes, your broad shoulders, the way you recited poetry after a few drinks.

"The waves in his hair are making me seasick," my aunt said with a wink when I pointed you out in the King's Head two weeks before the ceremony. We were sitting in a booth, sipping Pimms, while you and my father knocked back pints at the bar.

We left you both bellowing songs from the old country, arms slung around each other's shoulders, rapturous faces turned up towards the yellow smoke stained ceiling. Walking home through the Kilburn streets, I could feel my already thickening waist strain against my dress.

Bad omens one and two were the quick slaps you gave to my face a few days before we exchanged vows, the sound of them on my cheeks like something snapping, something coming apart, something tearing at the seams.

Nicola Godlieb

70th, Down the Anchor and Hope

By eight pm he's poured 90% proof rum on his shorts, set them on fire and hit the ground running.

He clocks Nance, cackling, in her breakable strappies, her moth-kibbled parrot perched, voice tinny and upturned. *Beer eh? Beer eh?* Cock-a-snook to raise her glass, the bird juts a crackled grey tongue, flicking the froth up lizardy-quick, winking its cataract eye. He belts past the rockabilly band, off-beat and cycle-powered by a sandalled kid in peach bunny ears, mouth spit-brimming for tomorrow's Sherbet Dib-Dabs.

Whooshing cinders like cock feathers he's now past the church, closed, as he knew it would be, its stained glass soldered back in like a jammed kaleidoscope. In the road, plastic wrappings wind diaphanous and it's almost his childhood river, with its ancient breeds of grazing cattle, in mirage, once a year. Creeping marshwort and Skipper butterflies. Pyraloid moths and creased crested newts that would nuzzle at his thumb. A breeze blows restless through his limbs, and, sudden as the sound of grasshoppers it comes, in a glorious scraping cacophony, that there's something he's lost in the fold of the years; a kiss from his mother and her fingertips light to the back of his head, and *Nothing's Impossible, Pet.*

At early hours A&E they pack his genitals with cream and padded gauze, and by lunchtime he's taped together, back at the pub, his pint-eyes fixed on his usual spot. There'll be nothing amiss until closing. A flock swells and shimmers in late green above the flyover, in möbius strip. And a pungent bloom of river weeds, though it's all city.

Elaine Mead

Probably Nothing

These roads aren't familiar to us and the landscape is uneventful. The occasional grey blur of a sheep darts across a field as we speed past, emerging like a mirage, shimmering into focus. Blending back just as quickly.

The sun is at its peak, nipping your hands on the steering wheel, making my bare knees hot. *Biting* you call it and the expression stays with me for years.

Just as the boredom kicks, the scene slowly changes. Dense thickets of woodland begin to rise up as you follow the curve of the road. Trees soar skyward on either side of us, offering a shower of shade, the coolness a welcome slice. Momentarily distracted, neither of us sees the animal dart out across the road.

You hit the brakes hard, reach one arm across in front of me. Protective. The creature lurches away.

"Close one," you exhale in one forced breath.

"What was that?" I search the bush, scanning between the trees.

"A kangaroo?" The car engine idles.

"It looked more like a dog," I turn to face you.

Your reply is quashed by movement on the road behind us. I watch your brow furrow as your eyes scan the rearview mirror. A man has emerged from the trees, standing in the road not far behind the car. I can't make out his expression.

He points at us.

"Should we?" My hand on the door handle. Still watching the man you slowly accelerate, moving us away. Subtly shake your head.

"Probably nothing."

Jenny Cozens

Break out

I stir in the sugar and watch my phone blinking at me, winking that I'm needed. His photo's glued to the back, ringed by the diamante heart that Helena suggested. It's not permanent; not like tattooing his face on my right buttock as he'd wanted, but still it shows commitment.

Sarah's drinking water. No money for coffee and she won't borrow. The text is from her mum, the usual sort of thing: "Don't forget Sammy has to eat too. Eggs, but maybe no bread. Might be something in the freezer." She's wearing the bright pink jumper she bought at Oxfam, its colour screeching at us and changing the table's shiny brown Formica into candyfloss.

Natalie sits opposite, blue-nailed, blue-jeaned, thick brown hair hiding her face as she reads her Facebook messages. Unsmiling and hunched, her coffee's cold by now. Perhaps they're sneering again: "Still wearing your ugly, grey cardie Natalie? Still thinking about girls?" Last week they told her to cut her breasts off. "Just do it," they said.

Helena's lost her phone and is wondering how life can continue. She's put herself in solitary, hair covering a face that's propped by angry fists. Perhaps I should be concerned, but his message is prodding and poking at me. Last night we fought: things he wanted me to do. And him to film. He was excited and I was spoiling everything, whispering no. As usual.

I stare at my phone winking away, demanding my attention. Perhaps he's suggesting a DVD at his place; or saying: "Bye. I don't need a prude."

I hug Helen and lean across to Natalie to turn her phone face down. Do the same to Sarah's and glance at my own, still flashing before I press DELETE.

"Come on", I say. "Let's run along the beach."

J A Keogh

Bread of Heaven

The woman in the photograph leans against the coal bunker in her vest and steel capped boots. Her short dark hair is slicked back but a natural curl springs out from behind her ears. A young girl, a tiny replica of the woman, stands beside her in the sloping back garden and mimics her pose. The woman is sucking on a cigar and the girl is giggling.

The woman in the photograph left school at fourteen to work underground and break some moulds. At sixteen, a mineshaft collapsed and she escaped with a small depression above her right eye. A depression that throbbed blue in winter and blushed puce in summer.

The woman in the photograph drank pints of creamy stout on Saturday nights in the pub snug, waiting for Dai The Lie to trample the ivories. Waiting to showcase her falsetto version of Bread of Heaven. On Sunday afternoons, she'd hide them all behind the mint coloured corduroy sofa. The silhouette of the debt collector at the back door, slowly retreating into the fading valley light.

The woman in the photograph sometimes took a bank holiday coachload on a magical mystery tour. Three cheers for the same exhausted seaside town and the dirty, coffee coloured sea. The shillings collected later in a biscuit tin. Three fish and chip suppers collected on the way home: no vinegar.

The woman in the photograph asked her indoors not to send little Edna in that morning, with that sprain.

The woman had just started the morning shift when she heard the grumble of the coal slithering down toward the school playground. Later, she had told reporters and television people that the noise above her had sounded like the very end of the world.

Which of course, it had been.

Niki Mottahedan

Because mama loves you

A pitter-patter of little feet, like an unsteady heartbeat.

Mama! Mama! Fly! Fly!

Romy is clambering onto a tyre swing, gripping chain links tightly and bobbing excitedly.

Get down. You're not old enough.

I got us here before crow's caw on a Sunday, evading mothers' small talk and fathers' big talk, but not a gargoyle. Its hunched, paunchy body, sitting one end of a seesaw, gets up, totters towards us, becomes a homeless, hungover man, wearing: a stained undershirt, grey shorts, tatty flip flops and glistering sweat.

Staring down vacant eyes, sure he must be hollow inside.

This is a children's playground. I don't think this is somewhere you should be.

My swing, he replies, pushing Romy off.

Scooping up a teary Romy from the dirt, I swell with anger.

What the hell are you on? Come near us and I'll call the police!

An older couple hurry over, take in the scene: a man on a tyre swing, Romy's grazed knees and tear-stained face, my mobile held at the ready.

We're so sorry. Our son is unwell. It's usually empty this early, the woman pleads, then brushes past us, to where the usurper is swinging back and forth.

Come on, joonam, time to go. She speaks softly, a mother, listening for an unsteady heartbeat. Her husband only sizes me up against my talk.

Becoming a protective guard, they enclose their son in their ranks, lead him towards home. Soapy water is splattering the grass. Romy is blowing bubbles, bright as glass. As they fly over the vacant playground, beyond fluorescent gates, I recognise his voice, frantic, then faltering.

Look! Mama, look! Fairies!

Why Mama cry?

C.M. Davis

Dawn on the river at Benares

It had been the most sleepless of nights, followed by the coldest of dawns, and now this white girl wanted to take his photograph.

His heart sighs, but his stomach has the upper hand. *Play the game*, it says. *I'm hungry.*

"*Fifty rupees for photograph.*" Worth a try.

"*Haa, achaa.*" *Yes, okay.* She pronounces her *haa* correctly actually, through the nose.

Click, click. Click.

"*Sundar,*" she says, and hands him a note. *Handsome.* He laughs. When he looks down at his hand, she's given him a hundred.

It must be coming up for six because the darkness is lifting. The before-business men are arriving, murmuring, shivering. Scrubbing shining faces in the sacred water. The paunchy chai seller warms himself over the steaming pan, devoted only to a good day's sales. Now the ladies make their way, to wash and pray in red, blue, purple, gold. Where is the beautiful one, the one with the garland of marigolds and the oil lamp? The white girl is blocking his view.

She pauses. Does she expect insightful advice? Enlightenment? At this time in the morning? "*Hope nice photo*," he says as she smiles and she goes.

Over the years, he thinks, he must have been photographed a thousand times. How many faces does he have, out there, in the world? Peering down on middle-class families from sitting room walls? Gazing mysteriously out of coffee table books – the Wonders of India. Perhaps he's the most popular hashtag-holyman on Instagram. Or did most folks just delete him?

It is too big to think about. Much better to be in one place and one time only. Dawn on the river at Benares.

Ah, here she comes, like a reward for his thoughts – the beautiful one with the garland of marigolds and the oil lamp.

Wendy Turbin

Morendo

A busker on the prom plays violin. Wrapped against the chill, hardy souls gather to listen. Notes swell on the breeze.

Half a mile along the beach, Billy screws up his face. Dirt shadows deepen in the well-worn furrows. He flinches, but memories still come.

Anna-Nina-Princess on her seventh birthday, at the big bay windows, violin tucked to her neck. She stares across the road towards the sea. Her party dress is blue, with ribbons. Her mouth is set. She scrapes the bow across the strings.

A banshee wailing sings a better tune, he told her, or fingernails on chalkboard. Remember when Dad stood on Rex's tail that time?

He kept on till her face was shiny red, then offers a suggestion. Try strangling the cat instead. He'd probably prefer that to your noise.

Anna-Nina-Princess stamps her foot. "I'm telling mum of you!"

"Go on then. She's over the road, away from your racket."

"I'll make you sorry, wait and see!"

Along the beach, the busker's finished for the day. Billy laughs, his red eyes brimming over. He shuffles around in circles. Worn-out soles scuff through damp clumps of sand, arms wheel like wings. Thin wrists poke out from tattered sleeves. His coat had once been black. Now it's the colour of seaweed rolling in the waves.

Gulls screech overhead like bows on strings and Billy stumbles to a halt.

Anna-Nina-Princess went to church in a white box with lilies piled up on its lid. Workmen on their road stopped painting zebra stripes and bowed their heads.

On the cold sand, Billy falls to his knees, Bowie playing in his mind. Damp to dampness. Salt to salty. We know Major Tom's a…

A needle slides into a vein. Tears drip from Billy's chin but now he can't remember why.

Benjamin Joseph

The Tourist

We pulled his body cold, from the deep waters, and I knew the djinn had hold of him. He lay twitching on the hot sand and his eyes turned inwards. I stood apart as they stripped his wetsuit and tanks from him, and I whispered half-forgotten prayers.

The djinn fill these waters. Shimmering shoals of wild dreams and old magic. When we dived for pearls, long decades past, we would hear their chorus of applause as we drew their treasures from the depths. They clung close to us as we plunged through their realms, sipping the distant sun from our warm bodies.

They took men more often then. Those that dropped too deep, too long. Curious djinn would drift behind divers' eyes and slip with them into sleep under the waves. They might hope to be dragged desperately back ashore, to recover on dry sands under warm sun, eager visitors to the shimmering world of the shore. Else you might sink down, lost, into the secret places of the spirits.

These days the tourists don't dive for pearls. They wrap themselves in dark rubber and protective glass. The djinn shy from their touch. We no longer bewitch each other. Spirits run scared from the bubbles that spill from steel tubes and plastic. This one must be very young, to dream of such a modern world above.

The tourist survived that day. I saw him once afterwards, in the new white hospital on the hill. He wouldn't speak. The soft light from the window fell over his wide eyes. He lay so straight now, held between the plastic tubes and the breath of machines, and his panic felt familiar. I smiled gently and spoke to him in the old language.

"It's okay, don't fight. You get used to it."

Lyn Ellis

Tainted Pink

You stand there and expect to be taken seriously.

Your shape an unnecessary bulk on strawberry milkshake dipped legs so bandy they must be an accident. Your powder puff emulsion beak hooks grotesquely into patent leather black, matching the surprise of dark feathers exposed as you stretch out your eighties bat wings. Dated. But wearing it well.

Your feet fart as they mulch up and down on the water's claggy bottom. Your awkward beauty screeches of vanity but you have no qualms about diving your head into the crap infested water to suck up grubs and algae. You are unembarrassed as shit fires out in a mustard dart, sinking into the water that you have just fed from. Florida pink trash.

Your neck strains and straightens as you squawk. Your cry like a pinched balloon slowly deflating before being released to scream in spirals. You wrap that long essing neck around your puffed-up bulk, a pink question mark. You are a filthy, gorgeous contradiction. A kitsch ornament standing proud in an auntie's garden. An obsession tainted pink.

Soon you will know that an obsession discovered and shared is an obsession halved. Sanitised, primed, marketed. Force fed shrimp to maintain your blush. One in a crowd of many, shagging in front of a two-way mirror. Soon you will be perched on shelves, be stamped on notepads and balanced on the tips of cheap, paradise pink fluffy pens. Degraded. Cashed in. Dirty.

Soon you will bore them and be moved on, replaced by spitting llamas and hook nailed sloths. No longer spread out on duvet covers or trending on insta. Soon, all you will have is my private, tainted fascination.

You stand there and expect to be taken seriously. I stand here and expect you not to notice my wonder.

E.E. Rhodes

The Horse Wife

I've seen Mari Lwyd five times and each of them has tried me. Her empty eyes always saw more than mine. She fierce-rhyme spoke the words in my head, little words crawling, sitting in my brain-case. She knew the wyrd-ways and made me walk the path.

I met her near the mill where I shouldn't have wandered, seeing her there, where I shouldn't have strayed. She clacked her jaw and I felt my arm burning, unfurling words in a skin-punched yearn. She was lonely, she said, and wanted some company, and would I step out with her, in her black-smithed shoes?

I saw her by the Chapel and thought she might be praying, though the place was empty when the tin roof fell in. I thought I heard her laugh and a queer betrothal offer, but the minister from England said, don't be scared of a horse.

I met her at the Wych Elm where she was ribboned in its branches, even though it was my name deep-carved there. We all knew the hanging rumours of the darkness, but Mari Lwyd looks pretty with those ribbons at her ears.

I saw her at the door when I was leaving in my bone-box. All my stick body was inscribed with her words. The minister read me, tried to pray away the visions, and the chapel women tried to wash away my sins. But Mari Lwyd claimed me, to dance as her beloved, for she was greylag lonely between the year's veils.

I met Mari Lwyd a final time and now I wear the ribbons. Did no bodies say who our word cudgelling won? If only the Wych Elm had taken me instead. With each rhyme weeping, I tell you this truly, I'll be the ribboned horse wife now I'm dead.

Victoria Stewart

People in Common

I was in the park with Shona, and her friend Eliot stopped to speak to her, and said, "We're having a party to cheer Dave up. Come along." Eliot jerked his head in your direction when he said your name, to introduce you. You stood in the shade of a tree, as far out of the sun as you could get. You were wearing black jeans, black boots with pointed toes, and a black shirt, and you held a thin, white carrier-bag containing, I could see, a copy of Pulp's new album, *Common People.*

When Shona and I got to the party, I decided to sit on the sofa and talk to whoever came and sat next to me, and this worked well: you and Eliot had some interesting friends. I asked each of them, "Where's Dave? I heard the party was to cheer him up," but nobody seemed to know where you were or whether you were feeling cheerful yet.

Eventually you appeared. You were wearing black jeans, black boots with pointed toes, and a black t-shirt. You sat next to me, and I said, "Is the party cheering you up?" and you said, "Yeah," though you didn't sound too convinced. I wasn't going to ask you why you needed cheering up, but you looked sideways at me and said, "Took a load of paracetamol, went to bed: goodbye, world. Next thing, Eliot was waking me up, did I want to go for a fry-up. Collapsed on the way into the café, and…" You made a rolling gesture with your hand to indicate what came next: panic, a phone call, blue lights, white sheets.

I said, "Well, that must have been tough."

Then I said, "Have you listened to *Common People* yet?"

Morgan Davies

After the Raid

The dust was thick on my uniform when I came to. I looked around for Collins. He was lying very still and I went over to him and shook him until his eyes opened. His wet eyes looked back at me through the dust on his face. He sat up and the two of us crawled out of the shelter and into the sunlight.

The day was still beautiful. In the distance beyond the meadow, the sea was calm and the clouds spread shadows across the water. Collins looked like he was saying something. I pointed to my ear and tried speaking, but he pointed to his own ear and shrugged. The airfield was gone. The final bomb had landed on the step of our shelter. There were buildings still smouldering and I looked everywhere for water but could find none. Collins dragged three bodies out from the mess. He went through their pockets and shared the money with me. There were cigarettes too and we sat on the runway and smoked, looking out towards the meadow.

Later, Collins found a pair of bicycles and we rode down the lane until we came to a cottage. A woman answered the door and we pointed to our ears. We followed her inside and she sat us at a table and brought us tea. We drank the tea and ate jam and bread. The woman brought beer and a photograph of a man in uniform. She set the photograph on the table and began to cry. We drank the beer from the teacups. Collins pointed at the empty bottle and the woman brought another. She was still crying as he poured it out. We raised our cups together and the dust fell from our sleeves and landed on the photograph below.

Alex Reece Abbott

Cool Cold

Hera inhales sharp engine oil, settles into the bucket seat and itches her bare legs where the cracked leather scratches, and – yessss! – heart pumping, she hears the creak and groan of the magical black hood folding behind her like a concertina even though it's a grey Easter day and she watches her cousin's strong brown hands gripping the sports steering wheel that reminds her of the one in her Noddy and Big Ears Christmas annual but this adventure is hers, and gravel scrunching beneath the white-wall tyres they bump down the drive and click goes the metronome indicator click-click-click and they turn onto the sticky asphalt of the winding Scenic Drive, travelling under the protection of a buttercup yellow enamel AA badge on the bumper with the mussing breeze weaving her straight hair into tangles and knots and she can smell subtropical dankness, trees and ferns rotting and growing rotting and growing and she hears the shhhshhhhhhhhhhhhh-shhhhhhhhhhhh lullaby of the bamboo waving in van den Berg's nursery and she shivers in her pink gingham seersucker sundress because it gets pretty cold in a Morris Minor convertible under a rainforest canopy, especially with the soft top down when the summer has given way to autumn, but Hera reckons it's all good since the quarter-acre neighbours down in Hendo can't see to dob her in and she rubs her goose-bumps and grins – it's really a cool kind of cold, especially when she knows her parentals would never buy into such cardy-less silliness.

Stephen Daultrey

Mortality

In the smoking garden, there's a drowned caterpillar in a bucket of rainwater. It's black, upside down, gently curled in its centre, little legs propped towards the sky like miniature mountains on a twist of liquorice, each limb marked by a spot, the colour of faded caramel. This still-life tragedy lies on a base of red plastic, while the water above circulates a procession of dirt and ash and broken leaves.

I can't take my eyes off this larval John Doe and I lose track of time, wondering how it got there, how old it is, what species of caterpillar it is, pondering the names I could have given it, had I been able to care for it. Silly names like Dave or Barry or Lester, or imaginative variations like Boomerang or Toothpaste or Magical Mister Mistoffelees. We could have been pals, me and this beautiful bug, until I know it's been 15 minutes, because Daryl my senior operative is in my ear, reminding me that my break is over and to get moving because the jugular veins of the pigs in sector three aren't going to drain themselves.

Geoff Lavender

Melanoma

There's this thing I do when another driver pisses me off. I shake my head, more in sorrow than in anger, at their stupidity and hope they see me in their rear view mirror. He'd just cut me up, the bastard.

Anyway he's hit his brakes and I nearly go into the back of his BMW. Out he gets and I think, Fuck, I'm in trouble here. He walks towards my car and indicates that I should wind the window down, which I don't. I'm not stupid. Well. I am, because I forgot to lock myself in. He opens my door and and tells me to get the fuck out of my car. When I don't, he drags me out, one hand on my coat collar the other gripping my arm.

He's shorter than me, but well-built. He looks like a guy who works out. It's freezing and coming on to rain. He's just in his shirtsleeves and looks ready for a fight. I'm not, obviously. People are sounding their horns.

She appears from nowhere. She's petite and dressed like a paramedic. I conclude that she is one. She says, "Can the pair of you take this somewhere else. We're on an emergency call." Shirtsleeves tells her to fuck off. Next thing I know he's on the deck clutching his wedding tackle. She turns to me and says, "That mole on your face, I'd get it looked at if I were you."

Kristina Sepetys

Will this be on the test?

Misty's wearing mile-high red glitter platforms and a pink child's track suit with a broken zipper. She probably pulled it out of a lost and found.

"Come home with me after school?" she asks.

"I guess."

"You don't have to."

"I didn't mean it like that."

We catch a bus. Transfer twice. Walk to a worn-out apartment building. Two men inside a dark car parked in front shift in their seats. One reaches for a coffee cup in a holder stuck on the dashboard. Misty waves. They don't wave back.

"Who's that?"

"In the car? They're ICE."

"Like immigration?"

"Yeah. They hang around here."

Curling paper signs taped to the building's front door: NO BATHROOMS OR SHOWERS FOR PUBLIC USE. Used-up men sit near the entrance smoking. Arguing. Laughing.

"Hi Rochelle," Misty says to a woman seated behind a desk blocking our way. Rochelle has long, sparkly gold fingernails.

"Hey, baby," she says, handing Misty a sign-in clipboard with a pen on a string. She looks me over. A ragged old man sleeps sitting up on a couch in front of a TV, head thrown back, mouth open, arm protectively around an overstuffed plastic bag.

"Your Mama's not home," Rochelle tells Misty.

"Yeah, I know."

"You're not supposed to have people up without a guardian in the apartment."

"We're just gonna study."

"You need to work down here in the lounge."

"The TV's so loud. Please?"

Rochelle waves the clipboard at us. Looks away.

Misty unlocks a metal security gate over a wood door. The bottom is scuffed and chewed like someone kicked it. She pours Wild Cherry Pepsi into a mug from a nearly empty plastic liter bottle. We sit side-by-side on the floor against a bed without sheets. Work together on problem sets from *Algebra: Structures and Methods.*

Lydia Clark

Barbershop Duet

A boy who misses his father needs a haircut.

He asks the chirpy barber, whilst gazing at the traffic outside, if his father has been in recently. The barber replies yes, he was sat in the very same chair just the day before. The boy feels the heat of his father's burly thighs, and imagines their chestnut hair interspersed on the floor. He looks in the mirror, and pretends not to see the ghost of a bearded face in the reflection.

He gets a birthday card a week late, written in familiar, heavy-press hand. No return address. No suggestion of where he might be. The boy asks the barber, but all he knows is a pretty young lady waits for his father, these days. The boy pays for his trim and leaves as swiftly as he arrived.

Hair flops over his eyes and snakes down his neck, but he doesn't go back. He tries tying it, gelling it, but the problem is unavoidable.

The barber is happy to see the boy again, and asks what he would like. Surprise me, the boy replies, and the barber does. Your father has left town, he says, came in for a final cut almost a fortnight ago. The boy is glad when large chunks of hair fall away, when he is dusted down like a rediscovered portrait. He thanks the barber, and walks out feeling fresh and new, eyes opened to what he should have seen coming all along.

Niamh MacCabe

Walking In The Beautiful Chinese Laboratory Dream

On Week 7, I had the idea. As in, the universe gave it to me, and I was quiet enough to hear its whisper which otherwise would have manifested as whine of cat, or wail of ambulance.

I ordered online, with no concerns about the digital trail I was leaving. If anything, I was making sure it was poetic, checking back over my search history to see how it'll read. *9:03 Repose-Depot, 9:27 Fifty-Ways-Bye-Bye, 9:40 Paradise-Plus, 9:58 Eezee-Go, 10:10 Dr-Dante's-Medicine-Chest.*

I found what I needed from a Chinese lab. I checked the customer references (yes, should've been a clue, but, well,) and concluded that this, at last, was the job. The package arrived a week later, dropping through my letter-box wrapped in smiley-face paper, a courtesy that almost broke me. I thanked the postman through the door. Appropriately, and without malice, he didn't respond,

1. Taking twelve pillule, waiting one-hours
2. Next eight pillule, waiting four-hours
3. To drinking vial
4. You are sit-down
5. Personal-affairs in orders.

That's it, other than the small-print at the bottom which I interpret as: it'll be too late to write farewell letters or revisit wills, you'll begin to have pleasant hallucinations likely related to childhood/teen years, you'll probably consider that this is what's meant by life flashes before the eyes prior to your sinking like a worn-out cushion.

I did it all according to the instructions, the Chinese translated by Google to an odd English. I felt global; connected to my lab friends in China, to the postman, the ambulance drivers around the world scurrying to prolong death. I opened the window for the cat, then lay back, limbs cruciform, eyes closed. I may have whispered "Au revoir, cruellest world."

After nineteen hours of luminous dreams, I woke, to my surprise, alive.

Anne Summerfield

Brighton Pierrot

Dodo's on the piano, hammering out "Keep the Home-Fires Burning" while Florrie sings to an audience of three. Each show, she's hoping the bottle that Max passes round will come back with more than toffee wrappers and a grubby linen button. Her delicate voice competes with rumbling, the artificial thunder of a distant salvo.

Across La Manche, Florrie's cousin Tom is deeply entrenched.

Florrie shudders beneath her pompommed hat. She tries to project her voice like she's been taught, tries to send it back home to Smethwick to her uncle's bakery, where oven fires are burning and loaves prove like she wants to prove herself. Where she wrestled with Tom that time – *don't send me back to the front a virgin, Florrie. Don't make me wait.* Her voice soars with her escape from the smell of yeast and wet serge. When, *if,* he comes back, he won't find her.

Tom's sheltering in mud and muck, feet rotting, skin crawling, a hundred miles from Brighton as the crow flies, eighteen years old, no longer a virgin.

Backstage, Florrie rubs at greasepaint with a cloth. Her exposed skin is young and red raw. She doesn't want to believe that Tom was only doing what was expected, signing up, pushing her against the wooden kneading table, play-acting at being a man. The words of the song, its relentless sentiment, have turned her stomach.

Tom takes the curl-edged photograph from his breast pocket, kisses it. "Can't wait to get back?" his mate says. "She's a pretty little thing." Before Tom can answer, the earth shakes, splinters.

"Two farthings tonight," Max tells Florrie. "Could be worse." Florrie stares out at the pink sky above the Channel, shoots Tom dead with her gaze. It's not enough.

Emma Kentish

Giving Up

The dress is peacock blue, golden thread sparkling through it. I smooth it over my belly. The only one I'd found that I could cram myself into, more suitable for a beach wedding, bare feet and floating hair. Instead it's a December morning at the Registry Office and I'm waiting on the steps for Mo. There's a conveyor belt of couples shunting up and down, factory perfect.

I long to smoke but don't have the courage to face the censure if I light up in public. I don't even have any. It's been a year since my last one, but the craving hasn't lessened. I dream about smoking, losing a lit cigarette in the bed and waking in a panic, slapping around the bedclothes knowing it's somewhere smouldering in secret.

Last night I'd slept at my mother's, mimicking convention. It was early but she'd already opened the second bottle. I can't do this Ma, I don't want to marry Mo. She looked at me through the smoke of her cigarette, appraising and cool, as if I was something she probably wasn't going to buy. Then she felt bad and tried to be kind. Have a glass of wine, go on, the baby likes it. You can have one fag, it won't hurt. I smoked all the way through when I was expecting you.

Another smug spliced twosome moves down the staircase and through the front door into the wintry day, hazy with traffic fumes.

Ma is to be my witness. I was married here she says. Twice. When I cry, she regrets it. She says there's still time to get to the tobacconist before Mo arrives. She's wrong about that too, Mo is coming up the steps. You know I've given up I say, putting her straight.

Matt Kendrick

Conchie Faces the Squad

I chew through commandments as we're mustered from the dales. No other gods, no idols, thou shalt not kill. Sergeant barks. The others fall in line. I fix his stare. He pins me down, digs in the shears till he draws blood.

Then, shornie, shivering, alone on the snow-fleeced fell, I'm made to watch. The others are put to marching – left, right, left – and fighting, twisted horns clatter and catch.

When they break for grazing, a tup smuggles me cow parsley. Sergeant hobbles him. The others keep their heads to the grass.

Sun goes down. I stand here all night. Hunger in my bellies. Cold bites like a wolf.

In the morning, Sergeant brings me a parcel in khaki. A uniform, repugnant yet tempting. I step slowly forwards then step slowly back.

The others have been mobbed into Swaledales digging ditches, Wensleydales chewing through barbed wire. On their afternoon cross country, they kick the khaki parcel towards me. Just put it on, they bleat. Some of them spit at me, call me coward.

The second night. The third. The fourth.

After a week, they drive me into a cage. And it is small and rusted. It is lonely. It is not bogged in mud and mustard gas like the fields they'll die in.

I dream of their deaths. I dream of biting the life from a helpless lamb. I dream of their taunt that digs in worse than the shears.

Coward. Clatter. Catch. Khaki. Thou shalt not kill.

The Lord is my shepherd; I shall not want. I stand, still and steadfast, apart from the flock. I do not quake at the shotgun's thunder.

Leonie Rowland

How to Raise a Tamagotchi

1.   Awakening

Your Tamagotchi is awake, and the world is on her shoulders. The housing market has crashed, and there's been a shooting in America. Consequently, your Tamagotchi is sad. Do not despair! Your Tamagotchi lives in a developed country and has resources at her disposal. Use the 'LIGHT' icon to begin her path to enlightenment.

REMEMBER: Darkness is a frame of mind.

2.   Hunger

We all wake up hungry, and your Tamagotchi is no exception. Luckily, expensive food tastes great! The shop is open 24/7, so she can buy whatever she wants, whenever she wants.

WARNING: Low happiness may lead to reckless spending— we all need comfort occasionally!

3.   Health

The Tamagotchi mental health crisis began in 1996. If your Tamagotchi shows signs of distress, discipline her using the 'TIME OUT' icon until she repays you with a smile. Alternatively, you can feed her sweets, take her shopping, or buy her a drink. If this makes your Tamagotchi ill, the NHS is at her service.

REMEMBER: A single smile goes a mile.

4.   Work

Our motto is 'out of the egg, into the job market'. Your Tamagotchi's mood may be low, but our expectations are not. There are plenty of jobs to choose from, but due to the high volume of candidates, your Tamagotchi is probably unqualified. Fortunately, she's female, so there's always marriage.

TOP TIP: Use that 'TIME OUT' icon!

5.   Marriage

The Matchmaker will appear when your Tamagotchi reaches adulthood. A relationship will ensue in miniature: hearts, fireworks, children. When the Matchmaker leaves, your Tamagotchi will be alone again with another mouth to feed.

REMEMBER: Surrender is the key to happiness!

6.   Death

Your Tamagotchi will die in front of you, which you may find upsetting. Thankfully, this isn't real life: press any button to reset.

Jamie D Stacey

Pizza in a lockdown

Pizza, she thinks, and dials 999.

"Hi, I'd like to order a pizza."

"I'm sorry, you have the wrong number."

"No, you don't understand. I'd like to order a pizza."

"This is an emergency line. If you have an emergency—"

"Yes. I'd like the pepperoni."

A soft beep. Her voice cut off. Her voice always cut off.

Pizza, she thinks. She's not hungry. She dials 999.

"Hi, I'd like to order a pizza."

"I think you've called the wrong number for pizza—"

"Please, I'd like a ham and pineapple."

"This is an emergency number."

A soft beep. Then another voice, behind her, eating her words and spitting them out. Later, her face like dough; kneaded, beaten.

Pizza, she thinks. She needs. She dials 999.

"This is an emergency line…" She tries. "…and this is not an emergency."

She tells him she dialled the wrong number, that she'll phone the pizza place now. Order his pepperoni and can of Coke, pay with her credit card. Later, she tastes pizza. That's what she tells herself; the hot dribble of tomato sauce running down her chin and staining her white top, the spots of black olive dotting her face, the texture of undercooked dough as she tries to move her jaw again.

"Hi, I'd like to order a pizza."

"This is an emergency line; do you have an emergency?"

"Yes… I'd like to order a margherita."

"I understand. Is he in the room with you now?"

"Yes… Extra cheese."

"Are you hurt?"

"Yes… Lots of cheese. You understand?"

"I understand. Give me your address."

"Thank you. It's—"

"They're on their way now."

"How long before it arrives?"

"Less than 10 minutes before they're with you."

Soon she hears a knock on the door. Prays she can escape this time.

Anne Howkins

When Gravity Gets Out of Bed at Midnight

When we were sixteen, gravity was apples falling from trees. We kept our eyes open for shooting stars when we snogged boys on velvet summer nights, while fireflies skittered away from bats. The moon waxed and waned, pulling the tides, pulling our bodies to the same beat, filling and emptying.

When we were twenty-one, sitting on a cliff overlooking the sea, the moon put out the sun, and night came in the middle of the day. For one triumphant moment the moon was the star, and we wanted to forget gravity, and wheel and scream with the sea gulls, and roost with them in the sudden dark, while people clapped and cheered. Then the moon sighed and let the sun be the star again, and we threw crusts in the air for the gulls.

When we were thirty, my sister had a husband, but not a child, because her body forgot how to follow the moon. It found a different sort of gravity, a drought, a flood and then the detritus – all the flotsam and jetsam when the tide and her hope ebbed away.

When we were forty, and my sister no longer had a husband, and her firefly hope for fertility was extinguished, and the doctors talked about the gravity of her condition, she went back to the cliff-top to watch the midnight full moon gleaming over the sea. And as the moon pulled the tide higher and higher on the sand, and the bats flitted after twinkling dots in the warm summer breeze, she tested gravity for herself.

Charlotte Fong

Cake for Breakfast

It is a dull slump of a morning and Billy is only wearing one sock. He sits on the floor turning the pages of his mum's encyclopaedia, looking for the life-sized photo of the Queen Alexandra's Birdwing. It is the largest butterfly in the world and, when he finds it, he will press his nose to its body and move the pages of the book to make the wings flutter above his head.

He flicks through the solar system, indigenous tribes, and a diagram of the inside of Krakatoa until finally reaching familiar minibeasts and the caterpillar to chrysalis transformation.

The emerald wings of the giant butterfly glimmer against the grey living room. Billy lifts the book above his head, but when he tries to move the wings it slips from his small hands and catches just above his brow. He lets out a frustrated howl.

Dad runs into the lounge, toothpaste on his crumpled shirt and face half-shaven. "Billy, what are you playing at? We need to leave in five minutes."

Billy begins to whimper and Dad spots the cut on his head. "Jesus Christ, what now?"

He rushes over as Billy blurts out everything between sobs. How he misses his mum who would lift the butterfly above his head while he imagined he was lying in a rainforest. How he doesn't want to go to school where they say his mum's gone to a home for psychos. How he could only find one clean sock.

Dad puts his hand under Billy's chin. "Forget school. Let's have cake for breakfast. This afternoon we'll give Mum a ring."

Billy's cries subside and he attempts a wobbly smile. Taking Dad's hand, he picks up his mum's book and carries it with him to the kitchen.

Catherine Ogston

The Value of Stilt Walking

I can hear Marla's voice now, demanded our turn, over and over until it became the whinny of a marsh hen. But Ed was never in the mood to descend from his new lofty position and only laughed and stalked off. No one knew where the pair of stilts had even come from but once Ed got his hands on them he spent every second possible teetering on them, wobbling like a baby giraffe at first, falling into the dry grass until he got the knack of it. The way he spent days like that, walking about like an alien with long probing legs, drove Marla crazy.

My camera was always around my neck that summer and so I took a photograph of my two cousins, Marla standing there, her weight shifted onto one hip and her blonde hair falling down her tanned shoulders, like she was a movie star and not thirteen years old, Ed in the background on his impossibly long legs. She was smoking a cigarette, taken out of Ed's pocket in a useless attempt to vex him into jumping off those stilts. She had lit it right in front of him and smoked it without coughing once, while he only laughed and quickened his giant strides, gambolling down the farm track and back again.

I guess Marla would be surprised to see herself from all those years ago, now that she looks after seven children and often a black eye. Ed's gone; one bar fight too many left him six feet under instead of six feet in the air, mastering those gigantic steps that never took him anywhere in the end. I'm glad he got a taste of it that summer; the clean air, the view from up high, the stars an arm's length away.

Patrick Eades

The War on Dreams

His tail wags as he sees me. Ears pricked up, his brown eyes stare into mine, innocent and pure. In another time, another place, I may have fallen in love with this dog. But as he sits at my feet, on the cold marble of the airport floor, all I have to offer him is a half-digested bag of pills that were to fund my family's emigration.

The pills and I will no longer fulfil our purpose, we will sit and rot behind walls, casualties of a war neither side wishes to end. I never dreamed of being a soldier. I never dreamed of squatting over a DEA manufactured salad bowl while two grown men wait for me to take a shit. I will the acid in my stomach to burn and churn, so the condom may burst open inside and give me one last moment of bliss, before the chemicals race to my heart and remove me from this nightmare.

I open my eyes to the satisfied grunts of the officers. Bingo, says one. The eagle has landed, says the other. They smirk, and tell me I can pull up my pants now. No-one offers me any toilet paper.

They lead me back out in handcuffs. I spy the dog, sitting next to his handler, the collar tight around his neck. His tail wags again, as if we are old friends. I wonder what he dreams of, and where his mama and papa and brothers and sisters are, and which men removed him from them. He seems happy, in his new life, and I tell myself to forget Mama and all the others.

It is not so easy to do.

Donna Macdonald

The Last Tango ... with my ovaries

Someone could`ve told me, could`ve maybe hinted, but no. I discover as you have the last blast, the final farewell you have to be so dramatic.

I stand up and feel a flood of biblical proportions. I`m so onto ya. I unravel myself and find what I can only imagine a crime scene might look like. The massacre of Glencoe in the toilet pan. I stand up just for a few seconds and make my way to the sink. I turn and see a Hansel and Gretel trail of giant blobs on the white marble tiles. They start off small and insignificant, a sort of light coloured fruity shiraz and graduate to a deep, dark claret. These giant globules just keep dripping and splatting. I wipe furiously and tidy the scene. I imagine someone knocking at the door demanding to see the body. I up my game. I have double re-inforced giant pad jobs with string, disposable pants, the most super of super-plus and puppy pads.

You turn up in my life for seven days, maybe five, then you just disappear. I`m thankful for that, you only cause me pain when you`re around. Weak-stomached, haemophobic men are left faint at your presence.

You have been high maintenance all my life. Menstrual injustice. Six months without you. I put on my vintage black and white polka dot dress, feather boa and red stilettos. I parade around the garden in airy, fairy floatiness. In the background, Freddie Mercury sings about breaking free.

Sorry, did I stand on your toes as we tango? Did I nip you a little in strip the willow? I feel a familiar trickle settling on my red stilettos. The trickle is camouflaged from the outside world. I am prepared.

Gavin Weale

David Fell

I.

The flour: sodden. The salted beef: rancid. The ship's cat: strangely toothsome, but now bones.

They gathered on the fo'c'sle, silent. Nutmeg. Had to be Nutmeg. The only one who couldn't speak their language. He thrashed his chains as Trotter and Pike approached. He could see it in their eyes.

II.

They ate in silence. Once a day. They closed their eyes. They swallowed blood. Nutmeg lasted them ten days.

III.

They avoided the fo'c'sle. If they met there, they would have to decide again.

Trotter called it. Straws, he said. Again, all their eyes met and agreed. Crosse was nominated to make the draw. A fair man. He'd do it right.

They trembled as they picked. Fell went third and drew the short one.

He stood there, face like a beached trout, clutching his heart. He sank to his knees. The others fell silent and waited.

Recovering himself, Fell begged: *A day, give me but one day. Then I will go quietly.*

A silent pact was made again.

IV.

Night fell. Fell paced. The others crept below, bellies creaking like the mizzen mast.

Below Fell's feet, all the fish in the seven seas. Enough food to feed the five thousand a billion times. Above him, the heavens in all their glory. His lucky stars. A moon that turned the tides that rocked the boat that would bring them home.

He whispered it, again and again: *In the morning, I, David Fell, will be gone.*

V.

The sun rose. Fell sank.

Below, the men stirred. A cloudless sky. A crisp horizon. A distant mast.

The hullabaloo. The whooping and hollering. *Fell's saved!*

Underneath it all, a quiet voice. The darting eyes. The flecks of spittle.

A shaking of the head. A new refrain.

Fell's gone, it went. *Fell's gone.*

Kirsten Mosher

Look Both Ways

A green light signals that you can cross a boundary. We're at the park and my bestie's talking to this guy so much he's already joining us, but that's ok, the grass is green and spring and flowers and now he's asking if we want to go with him.

A yellow light signals that things are about to change. I say no, but she says yes, and then before I know it she's in the back seat of his red convertible, so I don't know what to do, 'cause I can't believe she did that, but I can't just let her go, so I get in and the whole time I'm thinking about jumping out at a red light, but by the time I got the whole escape thing worked out he's parking the car, and it doesn't seem like anything is gonna be as bad as that, so when he asks us to go in the restaurant I'm like okay, and then we can't believe he gets them to serve Sangria to us, plus it's so delicious, smells like cotton candy and of course she looks older than me.

Red light signals stop. But she's the one who's still too scared to use a tampon 'cause it goes in, even though I told her it was normal, she thinks it would be like having sex, but it's not like you can get a baby from a tampon, so after the Sangria he wants her to go over to his apartment and this time she hops into the front seat, and just calls out, "See you on the other side". That's when I walk home.

Karen Jones

The Tree of Knowledge: A Beginner's Guide to Telling Lies

Mum says we can't have the fake bamboo tree in Ikea, but we love how solid, shiny, perfect it is.

"I hate dead things," she says.

We buy the tree.

At home, she rolls her eyes at it and us. In our room we stroke its too-green leaves, loving it when we can be bothered, ignoring it when we can't, knowing that, at worst, it'll gather layers of dust, but never change – never grow or multiply.

We didn't buy a dead thing. It was never alive.

In the restaurant on our birthday, Mum says she's baked a cake, so no dessert.

"I hate waste," she says.

We ignore her, call the waiter. She stares, fumes, but she hates a scene.

We order profiteroles and cheesecake. "One plate, two spoons." We giggle. Mum hates two spoons. She especially hates me being us.

We eat the delicious, drippy mess of chocolatey, cheesy heaven, smacking, licking and kissing spoons.

At home we eat the birthday cake. We're sick afterwards, but there was no waste.

On Dad day, Mum says he's not coming. He's with his new woman and we've never to be with her.

We call Dad, tell him Mum's out, he can pick us up. When he arrives, we hide. There'll be a scene, like the one she thinks we didn't see when Dad caught her with her 'fancy man'. He didn't look fancy when we spied on them. When we draw him in our book, we make him skinny, with a big nose, a tiny willy, angry eyes, no hair and, sometimes, a knife.

Mum hasn't been herself since he left – she's gone sort of see-through. I'm only myself when I'm with Dad. I walk past Mum into Dad's arms. Mum looks so small. She doesn't make a scene.

Damhnait Monaghan

In my dreams, we meet at the opera

When I reach the bus stop, my mother's gone. Is she lying in that puddle outside the Opera House? Or did I lose her in the lobby, distracted by the man wearing one red glove and clutching a bible? Retracing my steps, I find her under the twinkling chandelier, crooning a childhood lullaby. I approach, arms outstretched. So close! But she floats through the window, lands on the pavement and drifts off to sleep beside a bald schnauzer in a tiny green tuxedo. I rush outside to embrace them, but it isn't a schnauzer after all.

Wearing my green tuxedo, I walk past the bus stop, distracted by the ghost of my bald mother reading a bible. I reach out, but my schnauzer tugs on the lead, pulling me away. At the Opera House, a bald man wears a twinkling chandelier. He floats through the window and hands me a red glove. Then he curls up in a puddle and drifts off to sleep. Faintly, I hear that lullaby. But it's not my mother singing, it's my schnauzer. When I bend down to stroke him, it isn't my dog after all.

When I reach the bus stop, one of my red gloves is gone. Is it lying in that puddle outside the Opera House? Or did I lose it in the lobby, distracted by the twinkling man under the bald chandelier? Retracing my steps, I find him, singing my lullaby in his green tuxedo. I long to curl up and drift off to sleep, but now my mother's outside. Her schnauzer tugs at the lead, pulling her away. I crash through the window and chase them, but it isn't my mother after all.

In my dreams, we meet at the opera.

When I awake, she's still gone.

Judy Koot

A Game of Toes

The clothespins pinch Marcus's toes. In the past, he'd lace the floor with push pins, barbed wire, even glass. His therapist thinks he's improved. Because, clothespins, right? People hang up tiny, downy-soft baby socks with clothespins, hang them to dry in a gentle spring breeze. What could anyone possibly *do* with clothespins?

"Would you say this is progression?" Dr. Virtue sounded annoyingly rhetorical during their last session.

He shrugged.

He didn't care to tell her the clothespins were metal—stainless steel—ordered from some cheap manufacturer in China. That he'd hit the buy button as soon as he read the review saying, "These f*cking things completely ruined my linens." That he didn't even read the other one-star reviews, because it was all he needed to know.

Now, the clothespins are crowning his toes, gleaming in the harsh morning light spilling through the windows. He's walking through his condo, playing his version of Russian foot roulette—dare to walk long enough and something is bound to go off, is the name of the game. And today, he's taking his time: ten minutes instead of the usual five. Ten minutes, before he has to leave for office. Ten. Whole. Minutes.

Empires have fallen in less.

The metal *click-click-clicks* against the flooring.

His toes start to hurt. Really hurt.

He fears something might happen.

He fears nothing might.

Five minutes and thirty-seven seconds in.

A sharp pang shoots up one of his digits.

Then another.

Finally.

He stumbles through the living room, leaving a trail of red blots on the expensive hardwood floor.

He'll keep on walking until the time is up: Marcus, a knight in his own messed-up version of spurs, taming the invisible beast within, conquering who knows what.

Feeling on top of the world—until he doesn't.

Jay Gilbert

Kit

You made it almost a week before, in a moment of distraction, you asked for Kit. Stupid. You'd let your guard down, and his name spilled out like milk from a dropped jug. Not much to it, after all, just three little letters, but you'd managed to keep it all these years where it belonged. Under your tongue, couched in the cavern of your mouth for safe-keeping. You'd never let it slip before. That was when you knew you really were going funny, that day.

They went immediately for the binder. They have one for everyone, places like this: the sort of book you think St Peter might whip out at the gates of heaven, if you ever make it there. The story of your life in repeat prescriptions and lists of your grandchildren. Kit's not in it. They say his name back to you and you want to rip it clean off their tongues.

Kit. You used to mouth the word into his clavicle, thinking that only Kit would be *Kit* and not *Chris* and that his skin had the salt taste of a night on Tynemouth beach; of home. You drowsed with him there on the Long Sands and his tongue stole into your mouth like a thief.

Visitors Are Welcome At Any Time, but Tom always comes on Sunday afternoons when the building still reeks of boiled vegetables. "They say you've been asking for Kit, Grandad," he says. "Someone I should know?"

Kit shivers down your spine, prickles across your scalp. You tuck his name back into your mouth again, shelter it with your teeth. "No," you say. "You know what I'm like. Slip of the tongue."

Debra Waters

Make-up

Mum's lying on the sofa when I get in from school, half-shrouded by blankets. She hasn't been up for weeks. Her brain ticks over, stunned by uppers, dulled by downers. Her neurons call to her muscles to walk, talk, chew but the messages dissolve into nothing, like faces in fog.

There's no point asking her about her day, though she raised me to. While I'm skipping maths and smoking behind the art block, carers bathe her, friends nourish with Complan. Dad plumps pillows, tells jokes, kisses her. "In sickness and health," he says.

I don't sit with Mum because her failing body infuriates me; it should be sorting laundry, gossiping on the phone, fetching me from netball. I don't talk because my thoughts are jaundiced with rage, I don't hold her hand because my hands are fists.

But today I'm brave enough to be nice. "Auntie Pauline's visiting," I say. "Shall I do your make-up?"

"Yes please," she croaks.

I fetch her vanity bag – the inside is rusted with bronzer.

"Avon calling."

I glide blue powder across her eyelids – it's darker on the flaky patches. The cream blusher looks like a cracked river bed so I smear Vaseline on her cheeks then apply pink frosted lipstick.

"I'm studying *Romeo & Juliet* for GCSE English," I say.

"I like that story," she says, swallowing slowly.

"*Romeo & Juliet*? It's stupid," I scowl. "Innocent people die because some messages don't get through."

I storm upstairs, lie down, and stare at the Artex ceiling – I see a tree, a knife, a bolting horse. I pick a scab and watch the blood blossom.

When I return, Mum's crying. I stare at our reflections in the TV. I don't recognise us.

"Juliet's pathetic," I say.

Mum looks at me and smiles. "She's young," she says.

Alyson Porter

Shortage

In propitiation—in friendship!—I bring The Hairdresser my allotment of ice. In her tiny, sulfurous salon, damp with syrupy light, I'm always the only customer. Thirty-year-old magazines—brittle, brazen with Plenty—fan upon the tabletop. Alas, never a wait.

Lately she pumps me up until I'm high and wobbly in the swivel chair, captive in a ratty black cape that conceals my crossed fingers, then brandishes long scissors, playfully making dangerous little air-snips around my ears, and tries to sell me things.

Initially: expired creams, mousses, gels.

Nowadays: unidentified powders from stacks of blue plastic canisters.

But! Rituals, sharp scissors, friends—all scarce in these times.

Sometimes I:

A) capitulate.

B) remember to say: "Still have lots back in the Shelter!" (See A.)

C) change the subject—where DOES keratin come from?!

We keep edging brighter, more sculptural: something a potential True Companion might notice across vast cyberspace, like some rare flower blooming in the desert, when the Bosses aren't looking.

No Shelter for The Hairdresser. Just a salvaged yurt way out on the mesa. No government water—just a big rain cistern, patient as a god. Think fire-anthills. Months-old footprints. Trackers. Solar arrays, wind farms, megachurches encroaching—all in the lucrative business of capture and conversion.

The desert gulps down her paper plates, plastic-ware. The antique shampoo sink provides rusty rinses for her sponge baths. A rehabilitated oil tanker trucks out her drinking water each month.

I don't know how long this can continue. Sure enough, one day when I slip away from my daily ad-reading quota to see her—violet clouds finally towering in the west, a stampede of gritty wind!—her hand-painted sign is gone, the place locked up with a heavy chain, and through the window, all I can perceive is a flooding emptiness.

Annie Q. Syed

Alphabets of War

The rain, a river set loose, poured through the hanging plants and onto the gravel. The smell of the sky inside the earth made Yasmine remember the monsoons of her childhood in a country far from her immediate memories. Except it hadn't rained in months. The drought had brought with it temperatures that made a person feel trapped inside their thinking. Yasmine felt heavy, stuffed, an old coat that no longer fit around the waist as it once had. Thinking about yesterday afternoon felt like picking chewed food between her lower left molars.

She had welcomed a man inside her home who came from the neighbor's—she didn't know if he was a worker or visitor there—to tell her something or other about her fence door. "Come inside, please," she had said. He followed, thinking she needed something fixed, to him she appeared the kind of woman who couldn't fix things on her own. She took off her headscarf once she had closed the door. They talked about the weather, her kids, his business, and after making love, they lay on the bed, she on the side that used to belong to her husband.

"I always wanted a ceiling fan," Yasmeen said looking up. Eyes closed she imagined a planetarium with rotating planets and stars.

They exhaled together, hands barely touching. He had strong fingers, a man's fingers, Yasmeen decided.

"Is that rain?" Yasmeen turned her head to the window.

"I wish," he replied.

"No, no, I think it is finally raining."

Nicola Godlieb

Aeromancy

My mate Soph has her jumper pulled down over both fists, cigarette in gob, trying to see how long she can keep it there. Like Clint Eastwood, her eyes streaming behind a fugue. Matty leans in, taking her whole fag in his mouth, breathing smoke from his nose. Then he stops my heart by turning and looking straight at me.

Matty has long hair and is always grimy with engine oil, sweat the tang of licorice. He wears eyeliner and has every inch of his right ear pierced. His name is all over the school, scrawled in an angular rock font and he seems to exist only in the corridors. After my routine break-time pummelling by older girls, I walk up to his name on the playground wall and scrawl above, I LOVE. He is pretty. He is 3 years older and out of my league.

But we walk, play hookey. Neck and talk philosophy. Find a dead pigeon, its guts shiny and pale under drizzle. Pin-pricks of rain infinitesimal on the high-rise concrete car-park.

"It's weird how you never see a bird as it actually dies, like, dropping out of the sky." He says.

"We should bury it."

Yet there's no earth. We cover it with what we have in our pockets, jelly sweet wrappers and Parma-Violets, some ancient leaves from the stairwell. The clouds above us flicker.

When I look back at us in this moment, kissing over an unloved dead bird, I remember the sparks at our lips, the strands of our hair standing up on end, something to do with the incessant mist of northern rain and the pylons that picket the town's perimeter. Electrons pulsing through us and up towards the sky.

Rose Collins

you will start from here

The sight of gummy eggs on a plastic tray was enough to make you weep. Pathetic, rubberised, the toast cringing underneath. The woman who usually brought round the tea presented them and, like with the tea, you felt you had to say thank you and not turn your face to the wall.

Sitting up was a problem. In the end the tray-lady helped. While giving you a gruff heave she managed to bump the side of the cot and it sailed across the room, carrying the scrap of baby with it. He was off, scooped in his see-through plastic hull, hoisting the cellular blanket flag. You thought of his little organs – like the pulp of stewed crab apples clutched in a jelly bag – and of his tender fish bones and sea snail fingers coiled at the temples. The head! Mind the baby's head, you thought as the cot smacked the wall.

Egg smell in the room like childhood, like sink water, like anaesthetic. Eyes down while a nurse came in and the baby was lifted up, buttery soft, and coddled! You laughed to yourself. The colour of them – sulphur-yellow, unnatural, deadly. There was a hollow twang at the centre of your abdomen, a pulse – could it be hunger? – the surprise peck of staples there.

The nurse hummed the baby down from squeals to murmurs. His face slackened back into its usual mode – watchful and slightly let down. She went to pass him to you but of course you had the eggs.

"It's breakfast," you said, and that was enough.

Rebecca Kelly

A Life Seen Through Broken Glass

Do you remember the broken panes in the sitting-room door? How old was I then? Four, five? The cracks radiated from the points of impact like spirals in an iris. Helen and I played quietly in the hall while you and Mum passed beyond and the movement of your limbs kaleidoscoped in the flaws.

Helen showed me how to wound our dolls. We used ink for blood, then bandaged them. Afterwards, we set fire to their hair.

It snowed the winter Mum fell ill. Helen and I laid our dolls in shoeboxes filled with tissue, fed them medicine, and at night, I held them close to comfort them and waited for Mum to get better.

I grew then. You saw who she had once been, didn't you? You watched me all the time like someone searching for a handhold. You bought a new car and painted the hall. Once, I saw Helen through the broken door and remembered mum and the way her dress had spread across the cracks like a blood splat.

Do you think of her still? The way she combed her hair? The way she jumped when a door banged? Do you cry in the dark?

I remembered, finally, the night I left my bed to crouch on the stairs. The glass was a web behind which you shifted and re-formed. The sounds she made after her head met the wall – like puppies mewling and all the time, beyond the panes, you moved in a series of terrifying frames. Each time she whimpered you said, "I'm sorry."

Can you still see the empty pill bottles on the bedroom floor?

Last time I visited you, you had replaced the door. "About time," you said. But it didn't matter because I could see clearly by then, anyway.

Emily Howes

Not Him

"He called me a bitch and said he was going to throw me out of the window."

She was laughing, almost.

"It's not him talking, Gran," I said.

"Oh, I know that," she said.

They had found him an hour later in the shopping centre with his trousers on backwards.

This time, though, they hadn't brought him back to her. She had had to go, instead, to the hospital, which was not a proper hospital, but a series of rooms where men wandered in ill-fitting clothes, pissing themselves in wingback armchairs and crying in the sensory garden.

I sat with her. It stank of soup and nappies.

"He's never spoken to me like that before, not in fifty years."

"It's not him, Gran."

"Oh, I know that," she said.

In he came, on the arm of a nurse. Grinning, goofy.

"Tinker!"

He winked, and for a second there he was, a trickster, sweets in his pocket, an American jingle on his lips.

Gran was rising to her feet. "He's not – he's not wearing his own things. That's not his jumper."

"Tea?" replied the nurse, all wipe clean compassion.

"Hi, Gramps," I said.

"You've been sitting on the table all morning with a lampshade on your head, you silly bitch."

"Bart!" she said. "Barton!" as if he'd stubbed his toe and sworn by accident.

He sat. Something yellowish on (not) his jumper. Egg.

"What the…what's it doing…"

He stopped dead, his thoughts sucked into the air. His mouth slackened.

"He needs his clothes," Gran said, her voice tremulous. "It's not right. It's not him, without his clothes, is it?"

She sat in the plastic armchair, nursing her tea, and I watched her trying to fuse together these two things: a small trickle of saliva creeping down an unshaven chin, and Bart.

Michelle Hemstedt

Easy Prey

I pull ol' Herb out of his pond and flash my teeth at a girl in the crowd. She looks like Donna – dark hair, big eyes and a smile to rip the shirt off your back. She's staring, and, damn, those eyes feel good on my skin. Hot tip: you wanna get laid, get yourself a job wrestling gators.

Herb gives me a sideways look and lets me know he's seen it all before.

"Don't you go making me look bad," I tell him. "You hear?"

Herb has eighty teeth but you don't see him doing a whole lot of smiling. Ten years ago I pushed my luck and he had four of my fingers when I didn't get control of his mouth fast enough. After that I got myself a swagger. Figured if an eight-foot, six-hundred-pound gator couldn't keep me down, then nobody could.

Donna packed her bags, took the baby and left. She said she needed a man she wasn't afraid of. They're living in Miami now with some realtor guy, the kind of fat loser who pays ten bucks to sit on a gator's back for two minutes while his little kid looks at him like he's the bravest man in America.

When I pull Herb's head back and force open his jaw the girl in the crowd whoops and blows me a kiss. I deadpan her but I'm thinking about how good she'll taste, about hauling her fit body down under mine.

We've gotten over our differences now, Herb and me. I was pissed when he mauled me but I stopped holding it against him after a while. He was just a young badass who didn't know how to play fair. Way I see it, he should've done a lot of growing up since then.

Melissa Bowers

Small Glass Jars

It's not that the fire has always wanted to be volatile, but when all you know is what it's like to be confined within a kitchen or a bedroom or, worse, the bath, surrounding a ceramic tub while two people intertwine inside the element you fear most, and when you wait for them to notice you're afraid but instead they say, *You are just the ambiance, you are the scenery, dance for us*, so you flicker and bend and try your best to entertain them, to keep them warm, and when you are never touched on purpose, and when you believe you are so fragile that a puff of air will snuff you out—yes, even from a child, while others sing in celebration of your vanishing—and when you are stuffed beneath chimneys and choked and smothered and drowned, and when you are the one doing the work of the gas stove, boiling, sautéing, providing, only to be extinguished as soon as you are no longer of use, and when you've spent forever thinking this is all you can do, this is all you can be: a single flame expected to stay small and contained in your glass jar, and when you have never learned that you can be destructive and dangerous and that there is an entire Earth made of kindling just for you, then when you finally get a taste of oxygen—when you see what it really means to breathe— you might rage wild and limitless through the mountains, too.

Tracy Fells

Monsters Like Us

"Marlene won't come out," Frank whispers to me.

"What's happened now?"

He mimes combing his non-existent hair, swishing his head so violently that it tips right back. The stitches circling his neck have frayed loose again. Frank's been banned from *Sainsbury's* since his head toppled into the frozen peas.

"The hairdressers?"

Frank holds his head in place to nod.

"You don't want to miss Bake Off," I say, knocking gently on Marlene's door.

When it opens I can tell she's been crying because her good eye has slithered onto her cheek. Her beetle black hair, heavy as a weighted curtain, hangs down to her feet. Like her nails, it never stops growing. "Isn't it your time of the month, Chloe?" asks Marlene with concern.

"I've a few hours till moon rise." My hands are still satin soft. Beneath the skin hairs prickle, threatening to soon sprout free, transforming me into a walking fur-coat.

We all cosy up on the sofa to watch the bakers in the tent. Julien joins us, after sunset, in time for the Technical Challenge. I howl when my favourite, the cute redhead, has to leave. Though to be fair, her soggy-bottomed Showstopper was a disaster.

"Did you forget your face mask?" I ask Marlene about her failed visit to the salon.

"No, but when I didn't register on their gun thingy they wouldn't let me in." Digital thermometers are the undoing of the undead. "Then someone used the Z-word," Marlene sobs.

"The living can be cruel," says Julien squeezing her marble-white hand. "Silly, when they're just like us."

Taking Marlene's other hand in my paw, a growl rises. "No, they're not," I snap. "Humans hide their monsters on the inside."

Together we sit in the dark, muting the TV when the news bulletin comes on.

Kevin Sandefur

Trains of Thought

The other prisoners have photos of loved ones. Family, girlfriends. People they know. Ricky only has one picture, of a couple he's never met, standing in the great hall of an empty train station. It's tucked on the underside of my mattress, where Ricky can look up at it from his bunk.

He says the librarian let him take it out of a magazine. I wonder if he's lying, because that's what we do in here. I ask him why the librarian would let him do that, but he doesn't answer right away. In my imagination, I can hear the wheels turning in Ricky's head.

It takes a while, and I've almost drifted off to sleep when he finally answers. "Because I like the room," he says. "It's big, and open. It's a train station, right?"

"I think so."

"You ever been on a train?" he asks.

"Coupla times."

He sits up on the edge of his bunk. "What's it like?"

"You've never been?"

"Never."

"They're big, too," I tell him. "Comfy seats. Cars wide enough to walk around in. Get onboard, hang out for a while, and when it stops, you're in a different town."

"That sounds great."

"It is."

"I'd like to ride one. Once we're out."

"Where to?"

"Anywhere," he says. "They go lots of places, right?"

"All over."

"Anybody ever get on with no place to go? Just for the ride?"

"I guess so."

"I'd like that," he says. Then, "Would you go with me?"

I hadn't expected that. "You don't need me to help you ride a train, Ricky."

"I know. It just seems better than riding alone."

I can't argue with that. "Sure, Ricky," I tell him. "I'll go on a train with you." That's what we do in here.

Valerie Cutko

Seven Die In Borstal Fire

McConnahy sets fires. I know because I'm watching him. I'm watching him because I want him.

He lives in Radcliffe. He's lean, looks like a Greek. I'm in Wainscott with the slow boys. McConnahy isn't slow. He's clever, graceful, well behaved. He's here because his sister's hair was set alight with a cigarette while she slept and her scalp was burnt to the skull.

I've been watching him since he arrived on August 16th. He disappears after dinner to the playing field. He has set a small fire behind the equipment shed, one beneath the old bleachers, and one on the edge of the football pitch behind the brambles. He douses the flames from a water bottle then clears the ashes.

If I can get him to touch me I won't tell.

Stewart Arnold

Water

A sticky hot day watching Disjointed Ununited lose another game. Now the consolation meal. My pal Keith, his son Jake, me and my son Zach. Burgers, fries, drinks. Mine a coffee, Keith water, fizzy drinks for the boys. Cue school teacher Keith lecture. *Don't drink that rubbish, drink water.* According to the lads, water was boring and what we drank in the olden days before fizzy drinks were invented. Enter Keith for the Water Party; imagine the slogan. Go, *Go, H2O, turn it on and let it flow.* According to Sir, 70% of Earth's surface is water, the oceans 96% of it and the human body is three-fifths water. Farmers rely on rain to grow food. Oceans, seas, whales, fish; the list, like Keith, was endless. Keith asked *You both go swimming don't you.* They nodded. *Well, imagine Water Polo with no water.* I did; it would be Polo. Keith asked what is more valuable: gold, money, water? In Barrister-speak this is a leading question. Leading and loaded. Their answer, money. Why? Because with enough you can buy anything. Keith regrouped with a fresh offensive asking which they would choose if lost in the desert. To blank faces he triumphantly declared *Can't drink gold or money, can you?* Then the ultimate game-winning clincher, the little matter that Life itself depends on water as oxygen comes from plants which need water to survive. My arm had caught the waiter's attention. Was I waving or drowning? We ordered burgers and fries. Then, the drinks. I needed my double expresso so badly. Keith asked the boys. *Water please* said Jake. Proud Keith beamed like a lighthouse. And you Zach? I asked. He hesitated and replied *Chocolate milkshake please Dad*. Back of the net! A last-minute equaliser in another Disjointed Ununited day.

Rae Cowie

The Promise of Snow

Amber alert. Check before travelling. Several inches of drifting snow expected. Neve drains her mug of tea and rises from the kitchen table. No time to watch the flutter of starlings fight over yesterday's crumbs.

She grabs her car keys and sets off for the supermarket, which is busy for a weekday morning. She snatches a trolley, rather than her usual basket, stocking up on double cream and diced beef, fat shallots and sprigs of thyme. And wine. Six bottles. The colour of plums. Then she races along the home-baking aisle shovelling in dumpy bags of flour, slabs of dark chocolate and extra-large eggs. A quick check to ensure none are cracked.

By the time she reaches the car park again the air is a brooding slate grey. Surely the sign of a snow day. Soon children will abandon their classrooms to scramble outside in padded jackets to gather at the top of the hill. Whilst their parents will moan about cancelled meetings, but soon their laughter will mingle with the children's, and Neve will hear them as she stirs a beef casserole and whisks cream into peaks.

Then the weight of the hamper will tug on the small of her back as she tramps up to meet them. She will offer beakers of hot chocolate and flasks of mulled wine. They will cluster around as she serves wedges of chocolate cake, laughing as they say they should do this more often. She will invite them for dinner and, for once, she'll have company as they polish off the mulled wine and start on gin, making fun of her music selection.

Now the cake is cool and ready to sandwich with cream.

In the garden, flakes tumble and whirl in pretty pirouettes before melting amongst the mud… Then they stop.

Anita Goodfellow

Street Life

The father of my children is in a benevolent mood as he pulls me down on the earth beside him.

"Sit, Bina."

There's warmth in his voice, but it's still a command.

A skinny dog roots through the rubbish. The animal won't find a morsel – I've taken anything worth taking. In the mango tree a monkey bares it's pink gums, revealing sharp little teeth. The fruit is long gone. Beyond the plastic tarpaulin rickshaws rattle by, honking their horns and the diesel fumes settle like toxic rain over our makeshift home. The glow from the sun is warm on my back – the fierceness of the heat yet to come.

He lays his head in my lap. His hair is oily. As I massage his scalp he groans with pleasure. I smile. Days like this are rare.

Gita appears, laughing.

At the sound of his youngest daughter his jaw tenses. I shake my head at her, my eyes telling her to go. To leave us. To not shatter this mood.

She holds an orange aloft like a trophy. I want to tell her that *stealing is a sin*, but she looks happy so I keep the words inside. The skin is undamaged. A perfect globe. The colour reminds me of the flames from a street brazier in winter and of the priest's trailing robes. It's the purity of the blessing on my forehead, faded now.

As Gita skips over her father's legs his hand seizes her scrawny ankle and she falls flat on her face in the filth. He plucks the orange from her hand and bites into the flesh, spitting out the skin. The juice dribbles down his chin and my mouth waters.

Tears pool in Gita's eyes, but I know better than to comfort her.

Barbara Black

Geological Time

For a year now, Georgia had suffered from intermittent catatonia. It always kicked in when she looked at Mount Pedernal at sunrise. She was paralyzed by its geological brutality. Ralph—with his turkey jowls and age-spotted skin—leaned on his ash wood shovel and said: "Old woman brain. Seen it in my mother, seen it in my aunts, seen it in my wife." Right after he'd said this for the third time, a yellow jacket stung him on the lip, as if the natural world had opinions. Ralph was wrong, of course, just as he was wrong about everything, despite the conviction of his every utterance—from how to dig a post hole to why Jesus never wore wool. It was the Godlessness of the mountain that made her stricken. The mean geometry of it you couldn't argue against. Or praise. It put to bed all those notions about God's hand in the frilly interior of a peony. It spoke only of itself. It needed neither man nor woman to validate its existence. Throughout the day, it changed with the light, suggesting it might be otherwise than the moment before. It stilled her body and struck her dumb. There was no paint colour for that.

Bernadette Stott

The Tent

My father's voice stopped me as I tried to unzip the tent.

"Go away for a little bit," he said. Not in a mean way.

"Why?" A pause.

"I'm just having sex with a friend."

A throaty giggle from inside was hushed with a word, so I walked away, jangling the coins in my pink leatherette purse. The sun was dipping low to the west as I roamed towards the corner shop.

"You back again?" said the old man with the withered hand. I shrugged. He put my crisps in a stripy blue carrier bag, took my 50p and then pulled a strawberry lolly out of a cloudy jar and placed it solemnly in the bag. My head bobbed in thanks.

I sat on the warm top of a picnic table, my feet on the seat, and ate the crisps one at a time, sucking each one slowly, the vinegar puckering the skin on the roof of my mouth. I wished for my book, but it was in the tent. Exactly how long was 'a little bit'? I'd almost finished the lolly when Dad appeared, barefoot, mad-haired and pointing at my mouth.

"Bad for your teeth kiddo."

I left that there. He sat down beside me, his warm denim knee touching mine, his body making the wood sag. We stayed like that for a bit, me sucking the lolly, him contemplating his dirty feet, the light slipping out of the summer sky.

Then, "Sorry 'bout that, still getting used to having a kid."

I left that there too.

I bounced my feet on the wood, but kept my knee next to his as I crunched the tiny nub of my lolly.

Mum had never, ever said sorry for anything; so that was something.

Audrey Niven

Any fule kno, men chat shit

She says she loves him and you have to believe her because she is a complete stranger sitting in a booth with her back to you and you shouldn't be listening but what else can you do? So you suck up your milkshake as quiet as you can and eat your fries, and she says she loves him again, but then she says what *would you do?* And the girl with her says, *I don't know, I really don't,* and you wonder what the dilemma is and what she looks like and then she's saying *I've tried, I've really tried, but no matter what he does I can't get over the fact that he lied to me all this time,* and her friend says *you might not have found out at all, so does it really matter?*

And you're thinking what has he done, this fella? She sounds fit, the girl talking, like she has a nice top on and make-up, hair all nice. You don't go round dissing on women like that, man. That's what you would say if you met her fella.

She says *it's only for the kids that I put up with it* and her friend says *I know, bae, I know* and you like the sound of the friend too, cos who doesn't want a friend that just agrees with them, eh? You want that all your life, someone to go burger bar with you and listen to your woes and not call you out. She's saying *look we better get going, his mum won't look after them forever.*

You hear them sliding out of the booth and you just know they're gonna be honeys. Then they walk past you, just basic. And you think to yourself, man, maybe it's okay if he lied.

J A Keogh

Restore to factory settings

It's fair to say that we were obsessive movers back then. It was far more than a hobby to us. It was far more rewarding than collecting stamps or crocheting Arizona landscapes or mastering an origami swan.

We definitely weren't dancers; it wasn't that type of movement. Although we could do a pretty mean Foxtrot after a pint of gin. It wasn't turning the tins label outwards, or putting our vinyl collection in alphabetical order, either. Or running on the spot: that would have got us nowhere.

We were serial home-seekers. House, apartment, trailer or houseboat: it made no difference to us. Perennial deserters meet professional clothes packers. The Bonnie and Clyde of the East Coast rental market. I could actually count on the fingers of no hands the amount of times that we'd outstayed our welcome. The rule: no longer than six months under any particular piece of sky.

It was me more than him. Me: a frayed question mark; on my hands and knees, checking the grass was a deeper colour on this side. Collating the reasons to leave and secreting crumpled Post-Its dying into his lunchbox. Him: a bold exclamation mark in Wingdings; loud and sometimes confusing but hard to ignore. Stating his case for the defence: sounding as convincing as Nixon.

We naturally resisted social media profiles or saving any information to the Cloud. We'd been warned about that. The last thing we needed on the big day was unwanted phone numbers and e-mail reminders raining down on us.

Time to restore to factory settings, I'd say, as we headed out of another shapeless town. I'd always clap my hands three times for luck.

The present is hard to hold onto, like a cheap kite on a windy day, he'd always say. He always said that.

Author Index